THE WAY TO IMPOSSIBLE ISLAND

Books by Sophie Kirtley

The Wild Way Home
The Way to Impossible Island

THE WAY TO IMPOSSIBLE ISLAND

SOPHIE KIRTLEY

BLOOMSBURY
CHILDREN'S BOOKS

LONDON OXFORD NEW YORK NEW DELHI SYDNEY

BLOOMSBURY CHILDREN'S BOOKS
Bloomsbury Publishing Plc
50 Bedford Square, London WC1B 3DP, UK
29 Earlsfort Terrace, Dublin 2, Ireland

BLOOMSBURY, BLOOMSBURY CHILDREN'S BOOKS and
the Diana logo are trademarks of Bloomsbury Publishing Plc

First published in Great Britain in 2021 by Bloomsbury Publishing Plc

A catalogue record for this book is available from the British Library

ISBN: PB: 978-1-5266-1630-2; eBook: 978-1-5266-1631-9

2 4 6 8 10 9 7 5 3 1

Typeset by Westchester Publishing Services
Printed and bound in Great Britain by CPI Group (UK) Ltd, Croydon CR0 4YY

MIX
Paper from
responsible sources
FSC® C020471

To find out more about our authors and books visit www.bloomsbury.com
and sign up for our newsletters

For Mum
and
For Dad

With love

LATHRIN ISLAND

THE SEA OF MOYLE

SMUGGLERS' BAY

THE PORPOISE ROAD

THE HIDDEN CAVERN

THE SWATHE

OWL ROCK

N W E S

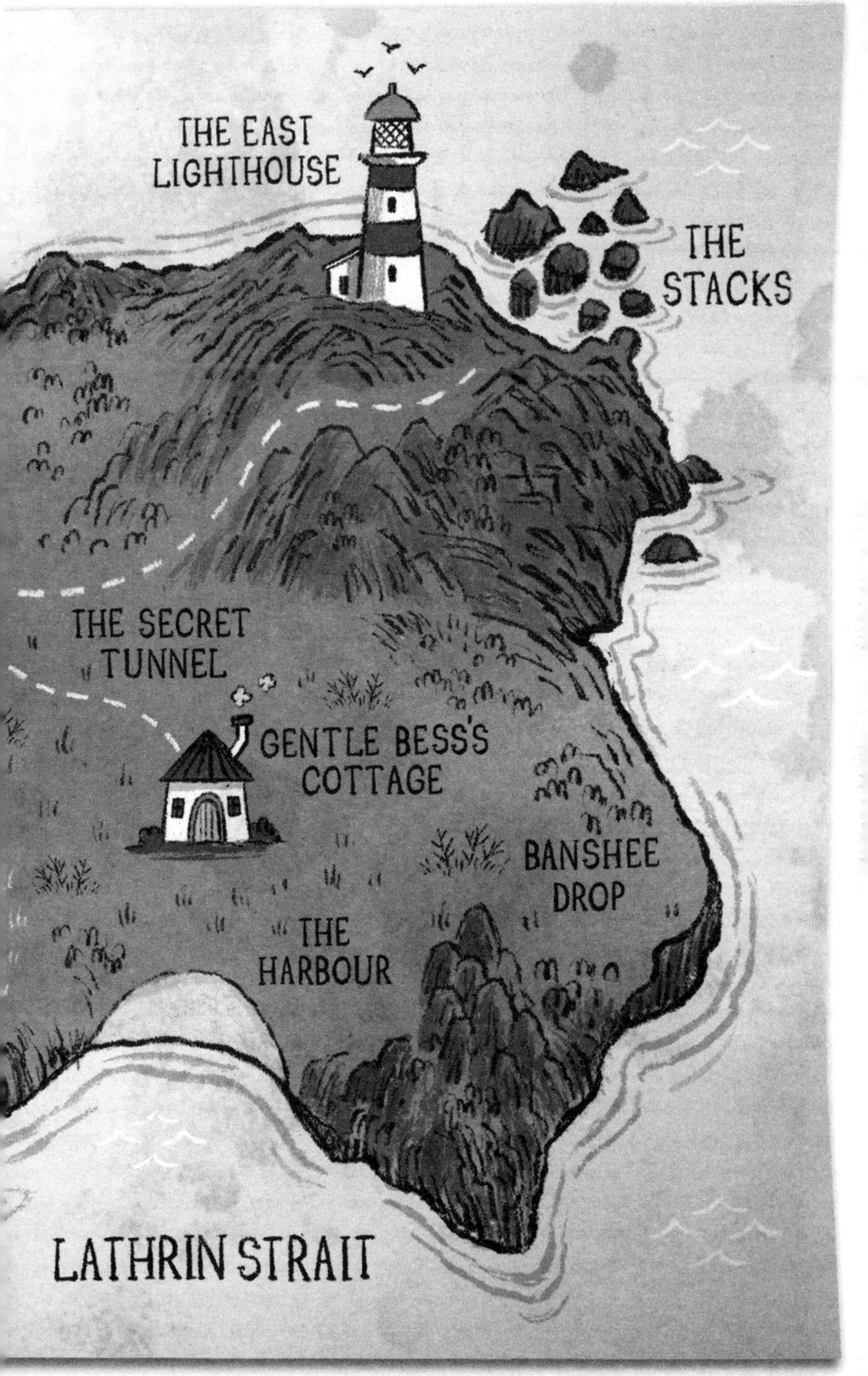

THE EAST
LIGHTHOUSE

THE
STACKS

THE SECRET
TUNNEL

GENTLE BESS'S
COTTAGE

BANSHEE
DROP

THE
HARBOUR

LATHRIN STRAIT

Come away, O human child!
To the waters and the wild

W.B. Yeats, 'The Stolen Child'

HART

Mothgirl perched on a strong branch and peered out across the wide green forest, hoping for signs of her brother – a wisp of smoke perhaps; the splosh of his homeward paddle in the river water; the high cry of an arrow-struck boar …

But no. Trees were trees, as they always were. River was river. Wind was wind. 'Where you, Hart?' she whispered. Her brother had been gone for two moons now, and although Hart was a full-grown man, strong as a bear, brave as a wolf, still Mothgirl was afraid for him.

From high in her tree, she squinted out beyond the forest to the Great Plain; that was where Pa believed Hart had gone, to the hunting grounds where herds of aurochs roamed. 'Your brother will return to us soon and we shall feast like never before,' said Pa each sunfall, but as the days and nights passed, Mothgirl noticed that even Pa's strong voice had begun to flicker with doubts. Even further off, beyond the flatlands of the Great Plain, Mothgirl could just make out the dark shape of Lathrin Mountain, jagged and bold on the shores of the Big Water.

'Lathrin Mountain,' she whispered. And she shuddered, pulling her white rabbit-skin close. In her mind Mothgirl heard the firestories Pa had told so many times about Lathrin Mountain and the restless spirits that roamed there.

'Oh, Hart,' she breathed. He had been gone too long. What if her brother had been snatched by spirits? Or what if strange clans had come, invaders, and taken her brother away with them to their far-ice-lands? Mothgirl squinted beyond that furthest, darkest place on the very edge of the land; her skin prickled.

A sharp yelp from the forest floor made Mothgirl's heart jolt.

She glanced down to the foot of the tree. It was ByMySide; he was waiting there for her, watchful always. As his amber eyes met hers, Mothgirl's wolf growled his soft warning signal.

Mothgirl listened full-eared; she could hear it too – the crunch and rustle of someone making their way towards them through the trees.

Swinging silently down, branch to branch, Mothgirl

landed lightly next to her wolf. ByMySide nuzzled his girl softly. She nuzzled him back, then, silent as shadows, they edged towards the old yew tree by the clearing and slid together inside its hollow trunk.

The air in here smelt damp and sweetly rotten. Mothgirl crouched down low enough to peep through a little hole in the wood at whoever was coming. It had better not be one of Vulture's clan, she thought; her eyes narrowed and her grip tightened on her spear. Resting her cheek on the soft warmth of ByMySide, she pulled the rabbit-skin cape tight around her shoulders, and she waited.

The rustling footfalls approached. Mothgirl breathed light, making ready to run … or to fight.

But as the figure moved into the circle of her peeping hole she saw that it was Pa. Only Pa!

Mothgirl breathed easy. She was about to emerge from her hiding place and walk with him, but she saw his spear was high – he was hunting. 'Wait, my wolf,' whispered Mothgirl, laying a steady hand on ByMySide's neck.

Just then a brown hare lolloped into the clearing – old and slow. Mothgirl's mouth watered at the easy meal; she felt ByMySide's muscles tense as he shared her thinking. They waited for Pa's swift spear to land.

But Pa's spear hand wavered, tremblish and weak as

he threw. Mothgirl's eyes widened in astonishment; Pa's strong spear had fallen foolishly short, like the spear of a small boy, not like the spear of a great hunter many summers old.

The hare vanished once more amongst the leaves. Mothgirl heard Pa swear under his breath.

She studied him closely: he retrieved his ill-thrown spear and walked on slowly up the hill: his breath rasped; the old hurt in his snake-bite foot made him lumber and hobble. A sudden truth hit Mothgirl, clear and sharp as ice – Pa was an old man now; his strength was fading.

A golden leaf twirled and fell. Soon the gentle green summer days would slip away and sharp winter would come; they would need to up and move their camp to the lake-lands as they did each year when the leaves started to fall. But could Pa still walk all that long long way? And what if Hart did not come back by next moon? They would need to leave for the lake-lands without him. Mothgirl's eyes prickled with tears as she imagined Hart returning to find a cold fire, an empty camp. ByMySide sensed Mothgirl's sadness and nuzzled her softly.

Suddenly ByMySide's whole body stiffened; his ears pricked and his neck fur stood on end.

A thin man ran, light-footed and shadow-fast, through the clearing. He was too quick-passing for Mothgirl to glimpse his face, but she could tell by his smell, which still hung bitter in the air, that the man had been wearing blood paint.

'Vulture's clan,' she whispered in disgust.

Why was one of Vulture's men hunting here? This was not their clan-lands! Angry now, Mothgirl slipped from the tree hollow and crept silently in the man's wake. ByMySide kept so close to her she could feel the soft tickle of his grey fur on her bare legs; he knew stealth like she did and his wolf paws padded noiselessly in time with Mothgirl's own feet.

They tracked Vulture's man unseen until he had passed back, empty-handed at least, to his own clan-lands in the next valley. Mothgirl spat in the hollow of his footprint, narrowing her eyes. If Hart had been here, none of Vulture's men would have dared to stray.

But Hart was not here.

Mothgirl swallowed; she looked towards the distant snake of smoke that rose from the trees across the next valley – Vulture's camp. Did Vulture and his men know that Hart was gone, that only Pa and Mothgirl and Eelgirl and Owlboy were here now? Mothgirl shuddered – if they did know, then that meant danger. Big danger. ByMySide growled low and long, like coming thunder.

THE STRAND

Dara climbed slowly up the tallest sand dune, letting the seagrass prick and tickle his bare legs. It was hard work; the sand was so powder-soft it slid down with his every up-step, but it was warm and delicious under his toes so Dara didn't mind. Not one bit.

Reaching the top of the sand dune, he rested his palm for a moment on his thundering heart. A gust of swirling salt-fresh wind flung itself at Dara's cheeks, like a whirl-about hug from a long-lost friend. He laughed aloud, breathless and triumphant. Flinging his arms wide, he let his T-shirt billow like a sail and he giggled again as the fast, wild air cooled his sticky skin.

Back at home the world felt all solid and real. Like it was held together with screws and nails and hinges. At home there were just the facts of things – he was Dara Merriam; he was twelve years old; he got up at 7.30 on schooldays, 8.30 at weekends; he liked bananas; he did not like pineapple; he always remembered to brush his teeth before bed and never forgot to take his pills. But here, by the sea, on holiday, all the facts of the world loosened and stretched and softened somehow. This morning he'd woken up at sunrise and gone outside in his bare feet beneath the pinkening sky, just to watch the world wake up, just because he could.

Dara grinned. Still panting, he gazed at the endless strand, a beach so big that when Dara was little they used to play that it was an actual desert; he and Charlie would trek across it pretending dogs were camels and even calling the sea a 'mirage'. Dara stared out at the grey-green surging sea, far too vast and noisy and wild to ever be anyone's illusion.

Squinting his eyes, Dara peered across the waves and drifting mist. On the far horizon, where grey sea met grey clouds, loomed the jagged, craggy shape of Lathrin Island. Wind-whipped; abandoned; wild.

'Lathrin,' whispered Dara, and even just the word made him tingle and shiver with longing.

After his operation, he was going to charge right down these dunes and run all the way to the harbour and leap straight into a rowing boat and row right out between the buoys all the way to Lathrin Island, single-handed, bold and brave. Dara had had it all planned out for as long as he could remember. He'd moor his boat on the island and explore all day, right until sunset, and then he'd set up camp and stay there all night too. Maybe, if he could keep his eyes open long enough, he'd even spot the Golden Hare. The Golden Hare – just imagine! A shiver of nervous hope and excitement danced up Dara's spine.

Dara took a deep breath. Still a little shaky. Still a little tight. He swung his bag off his shoulders, unzipped the pocket, grabbed his inhaler and took a puff. He felt his lungs opening like blossoms. He felt his heart ease. He popped his puffer back into the pocket, quickly checking that his little brass hare was still in there. It was; he gave the hare a squeeze for luck, like he always did. Then he swung his bag back on his shoulders and half walked, half slid down the sand dune towards the water's edge.

The damp sand was hard and cool on Dara's bare feet. He looked behind him at his footprint trail. 'Like a snail,' he murmured, imagining the muddly mess that the world would be if everywhere we went we left a trail behind us. Lines on lines on lines like a spirograph picture. He thought about all the trails that would be here; all the trails of all the people who had walked here first; yesterday and last week and his own last-year footprints, and all the others too, spinning back and back through time, right back to the beginning when every grain of sand was a rock and every rock was a mountain and –

The soft splat of a raindrop hit Dara's arm. He gazed out to sea at the ominous clouds rolling in from beyond the island. In the car on the way here Mum had said it might storm tonight. Dad had said 'But it never rains at Carn Cottage!' and they'd all laughed at that one.

Another raindrop landed, on Dara's cheek this time. Dara heard Mum's voice in his head; it was *not a good idea* to get soaked. He got his red raincoat out of his bag and put it on. He pulled his hood up and kept on walking. Rain pitter-pattered fast and noisy around his ears. He walked right out past where the hard sand was rippled like it still thought it was underwater.

Dara stood where the sand got sloppy and let his feet sink into the cool softness. He watched the out-to-sea waves rise up, fierce and lionish, before crashing down with a roar.

A brave little wave came rushing in, right over his sunken feet. Dara wriggled his toes and schlooped his feet out of their sand swamp. The rain was falling faster now, making tiny leaping ripples on the surface of the sea, like it was bubbling and fizzy almost.

Dara took three steps, edging deeper.

AAAAAAAAK-AAAAAAAK-AAAaaaak! taunted

a pair of young herring gulls, grey as the sky and wheeling on the wind.

He stuck his tongue out at the gulls and took another step; a wave licked the hem of his shorts. He'd love to dive right in and swim. Dara looked over his shoulder; he could see Carn Cottage through the haze of the drizzle. Were Mum and Dad watching him nervously through the window? Swimming on his own was another thing that was *not a good idea*. Dara knew that. He sighed, wishing he could do all the daft and daring things that everybody else did, or even just the ordinary things.

Soon, he told himself. *So soon. After the Big Op. Not long now.*

Dara anchored himself and let the waves rush in around him. Just a bit. Not too much. He gazed out beyond the waves, to where Lathrin Island rose like a rugged dream from the wide grey sea. He bit his lip. 'Soon,' he whispered, and Dara almost thought he saw a tiny flash of brightness dart along the craggy summit of the island – the Golden Hare? He gasped and it was gone; quick and impossible as a shooting star.

A sound came then. From behind him. The wind and the waves and the rain whooshed and swooshed and tipple-tappled so noisily that Dara thought for a moment he was imagining it …

He blinked.

Pushing back his hood, he listened.

No. He hadn't imagined it; there it was again:

A howl.

A howl so wild and lonely, the hairs on Dara's neck prickled and his mouth gawped open as he peered through the mizzle along the endless empty strand looking for a dog; it must be a really big dog to howl like that.

The howl came again, from somewhere beyond the dunes.

Dara shivered; this wasn't a *dog* howl. No way! This howl was different; this howl carved coldness into tunnels in his ears that he didn't even know were there; this howl rippled itself deep in his blood and echoed in his bones.

He felt sick. He knew it was madness, but this howl was a wolf howl. Dara was sure of it.

But it didn't make sense. There weren't any wolves; not here; not now.

Another howl.

Dara's heart fluttered like a moth in a jar.

He pulled his feet from the sucking sand and he ran.

HUNTING DAYS

Out there in the valley a lone wolf howl soared. ByMySide pricked his ears but he did not answer. Mothgirl was his family now; she laid a soft hand on ByMySide's neck; she smoothed his fur, soothed him. But Mothgirl herself was far from soothed. Out in the forest howls answered howls answered howls and Mothgirl thought about what winter does to wild wolves when the hunger comes. Vulture was not the only danger if they did not up-camp and move to the lake-lands for the frozen months.

ByMySide licked her ankle. She ruffled his thick fur lovingly. 'Wise wolf,' she whispered in his ear. ByMySide knew the most important things: he knew not to think too long; he knew to be ready and to be swift. And he knew that he was Mothgirl's and she was his.

Together they made their way to the riverbank, where Eelgirl and Owlboy played a game of jump-stones.

'My papa come back?' said Owlboy hopefully when he saw Mothgirl.

Mothgirl shook her head. She missed her brother, but Eelgirl and Owlboy missed Hart double-much. 'Your papa come back soon,' she answered in a certain-sounding voice, turning her face away in case Owlboy might see worry clouds in her eyes.

Mothgirl waded into the river to check the fish traps, but all were empty. As she stood in the cold, fast water, a leaf fell into the river and whirled off downstream ... to the Great Plain ... to the hunting grounds ... to Lathrin Mountain ... to Hart ...

She wished she could go, paddle her own canoe all the way to the Big Water. Perhaps she could find her brother; perhaps she could bring him home.

'Look me, Mothgirl! Look me!' It was Eelgirl. As soon as she knew Mothgirl was watching, the small girl skimmed her jump-stone across the river. 'One ... two ... three ...' She counted the stone's small leaps aloud. 'Ha!' she declared triumphantly to her brother. 'You throw a three-jump-stone, Owlboy?'

The little boy shrugged. 'I not want play jump-stones,' he said sadly, scratching a line in the mud with his toes. 'I not throw good jump-stones. All *my* jump-stones broken.'

Mothgirl swallowed her smile. Poor Owlboy; he was

the youngest, only four summers old. 'Here, Owlboy,' she called as she reached into the clear water. 'Look this – this jump-stone not broken.' She picked up a pebble, perfectly smooth and flat, and offered it to Owlboy. He splashed into the water and snatched it fast, solemn eyes flashing happy again.

Owlboy readied the jump-stone, but just as he was about to send it skimming across the river, there was a shiver in the bracken and a young deer sprang suddenly out from the trees. They all froze.

Silently, slowly, Mothgirl raised her spear, taking aim …

She threw true, but the sudden *whoosh* of the spear startled the deer, who leaped away and plunged back into the undergrowth, with ByMySide charging after. Whooping wildly, Eelgirl ran to chase the chase, and Owlboy thrust the jump-stone back at Mothgirl before he scrambled after his sister, waving his small stick-spear in the air.

Mothgirl slid the jump-stone into her waist pouch. Heart still pounding, she retrieved her empty spear and peered into the dim. She listened hungrily; if ByMySide caught that deer he would bring her back to camp and they would all eat well tonight. She longed to charge after them and join the hunt, but Mothgirl knew the

14

hour was growing late; she had better go home and blow the fire aflame.

As the sun sank lower, Eelgirl and Owlboy returned to camp, but not ByMySide. Mothgirl's cooking stone was hot; she scooped splats of nutcake mixture on to it so that they sizzled.

Mothgirl sighed, and peered out into the long forest shadows, her heart full of longing; this was the finest hour for a hunt, the hour when day turned to night. Mothgirl's skin tingled as she imagined running, sharp spear in hand, and returning with more meat than they could eat! 'Ha!' she whispered proudly under her breath. She knew that she was a fine fine hunter; Hart had taught her all he knew. But she also knew that this was not enough. Even if she were the finest hunter that had ever breathed amongst these trees it could change nothing; she was a girl, a twelve-summers-old girl, and as the seasons turned her wild, fast-hearted hunting days slipped ever faster from her. Soon Pa would say it was time to call her Moth and not Mothgirl, and her days would become woman-days only, slow and dull as mud, filled only with making nutcakes and scraping deerskins and smoking meat upon the fire.

A wisp of sweet smoke stung her eye, she rubbed it

fiercely with her fist and flipped the nutcakes. If Hart was here *he* would let Mothgirl hunt even in her woman-days. He would say *more hunters, more meat.* But Hart was not here and Pa did not think fresh thoughts like Hart did. 'Some things are done, Mothgirl,' she mumbled crossly in a Pa voice. 'And some things are simply not the way.'

Mothgirl hung her head; her anger wilted into disappointment. Perhaps her hunting days were already behind her now?

Since last winter when dearest Mole had gone to spirit sleep it was she, Mothgirl, who had prepared the nutcakes and bubbled the broths. Mothgirl's woman-days had come too early.

'Moth,' she whispered, trying the taste of her own unworn woman-name. She scrinkled her nose. It tasted unready, like a hard green berry.

Heart-heavy, Mothgirl gazed into the fire glow; she thought of things that are done and things that are not the way and her world clenched tight around her, like impossible vines. The smell, smoky and sweet, drifted up into the leaves, which flickered yellow in the gentle light.

'Nutcakes ready soon, Mothgirl?' called Eelgirl from her high-up perch on an elbow-bent branch.

'Ready when ready, Eelgirl!' Mothgirl answered grumpily. 'If you hungry, you go help Owlboy pick

16

berries. You six summers old, Eelgirl! You go fill your own belly.'

'Ha!' said Eelgirl, and she dropped a caterpillar on Mothgirl's head.

Mothgirl called out angrily as Eelgirl, still giggling like a chipmunk, leaped from the tree and ran up the hill. While the nutcakes cooked, Mothgirl picked hawthorn leaves and thought of Pa; a hawthorn poultice was good for steadying the breath. Perhaps with a poultice he could walk the long way to the winter camp, when Hart returned of course. As she filled her pouch with leaves, ByMySide came running out of the shadows.

Mothgirl crouched and held out her palm; the wolf came to her. 'Where is she?' asked Mothgirl. 'Where is our eating deer?'

ByMySide just blinked at Mothgirl.

Yes, sometimes ByMySide ate his fill first, but he always brought something home for the rest of them to share. That was just how they all lived: leaning on each other, needing each other, providing for each other. She rubbed her hand along his muzzle to check for blood, but there was none. The deer had got away.

Mothgirl sighed, her belly rumbling. ByMySide nudged her shoulder with his wet nose.

All of a moment Mothgirl smelt the burnt smell of too-cooked nutcake and she heard the familiar sound

17

of Pa's slow, heavy footfalls approaching through the forest. Mothgirl ran to tend the cooking stone and, just in time, flipped the nutcakes again before they charred. She could hear Pa's rough breathing now, as he climbed through the grove; nearly home. But why did ByMySide not go running to Pa as he usually did?

Mothgirl saw his hackles prickle as ByMySide growled softly.

'What is it, my wolf?' she whispered. Then *she* heard the other noises too.

There were different footsteps further off, and a hiss of whispered voices – Pa was not alone, someone else was following him here.

Mothgirl rose from the fireside, muscles tight with danger. She could not see Eelgirl, but Owlboy was near, so she made the owl-hoot signal, and when he looked to her, she put her finger to her lips; he hid himself amongst the brambles.

'Go. Find Eelgirl!' she whispered to ByMySide, and like a shadow he bounded off up the hill.

Gripping her spear tightly, Mothgirl lifted the skins at the entrance to the hut and slipped quietly into the dark. She hid. She waited.

BARGAIN

In the darkness of the hut Mothgirl steadied her breath. She listened as Pa's uneven footsteps approached their camp, then stopped; she heard the shift and crackle as he added more wood to the fire; she heard his weary sigh. Behind Pa's noises, though, were other sounds: snapping branches; rustling bracken; whispers coming closer.

'*Hoooweeeee hoooowoooooooo! Hooooooweeee hoooooooo-wooooooo!*' The bone whistle sounded from amongst the trees.

Mothgirl felt relief and dread swirl uncomfortably together in her belly. It was Vulture's clan; the bone whistle was their peace sign. Mothgirl lowered her spear, but she stayed hidden. Vulture and his men made her chest feel full of stones; they had sharp eyes which looked at her in a way she did not understand and did not like.

She heard the *crunch-crunch* of Vulture's footsteps through the leaves and the *swoosh* of his trailing long-cloak.

Crunch-crunch-swoosh.

Crunch-crunch-swoosh.

'HOOOOOWEEEE HOOOOOOWOOOOOOO-OOOO!' The shriek of the bone whistle was close now. Vulture's clan had arrived.

'Peace to you, oh great Eagle, son of Bear, son of Proud Elk of the Fire Mountain! Peace upon you and your children and your children's children …' droned Vulture's greeting chant.

'Fish guts upon *you*, oh stinking Vulture,' muttered Mothgirl, wrinkling up her nose; even from the hut she could smell the fleshy stench of the blood paint Vulture and his men always wore. Breathing through her mouth, she leaned forward and peered out through the gap between the skins.

Vulture was half the man Pa was. He was wizened and shrunken like a dried crab apple, but he made up for his tiny real self with a cloak of longest, thickest bear skin and upon his face and chest and legs he striped himself with blood paint. To his clan, he looked magnificent. To Mothgirl, he simply looked like an untruth. A stinking untruth.

'Peace to you, Vulture,' said Pa's voice.

Mothgirl felt the heaviness of the silence as Vulture waited for Pa to chant a long greeting like Vulture had done. But Pa did *not*. And Mothgirl was proud. Pa might be old now, and even though he was not strong of body, he was certainly strong of will. She knew Pa only chanted for spirit song, when his spirit was truly lifted or truly lowered.

Vulture was all noise and paint and untruth, and Pa was ... Pa was simply Pa.

'Come, Vulture,' he said. 'Sit by the fire. You are welcome here. Rest. Eat.'

Vulture looked at the nutcake Pa offered as if it were a steaming wolf dropping; he had no choice but to take it. Mothgirl seethed as he reluctantly nibbled *her* nutcake; all that hard work at the cooking stone had not been for the sneering lips of this painted fool!

Vulture laid the half-eaten nutcake upon a stone and spoke, his voice high and wheedling. 'Vulture does not come to you, this day, oh Eagle, to rest, to eat. No! Vulture comes with a bargain to make. Yes! Vulture comes with the promise of gifts: deerskins, meats, arrowheads. Oh, the great plenty, Eagle! Oh, the plenty!' Vulture stood up and thrust his arms wide. 'Behold!'

Bone-whistle music whined once more, making Mothgirl wince, but still, she was curious and she drew closer to the gap between the skins to watch as Vulture's men displayed their promises.

21

'Behold!' declared Vulture. A painted man knelt and unrolled not one, not two, but *three* deerskins, large and well-oiled.

'Behold!' cawed Vulture, and another of his clansmen swung a boar, fresh-killed and dripping, down from his shoulders to land with a thump at Pa's feet. Pa blinked, but his face showed nothing of his thinkings.

'Behold!' shrieked Vulture, louder still. A skin-bound bundle of cured fish.

'Behold!' Two fine spears. One carved with an eagle. One carved with a hart.

'Behold!' Twelve sharp grey arrowheads, laid one by one in a line upon a rock.

Then Vulture himself took a small pouch from his waist, and from it he emptied something into the palm of his hand, then gave his fist a rattly shake. 'Behold!' Mothgirl watched as Vulture poured the deerteeth on to the rock next to the arrowheads in a little white pile.

Still Pa just sat, motionless as a rock in a river.

Mothgirl saw a flash of frustration in Vulture's face. Were all these promises falling on unhearing ears, on unseeing eyes? Vulture drew himself up to his tallest, adjusting his bearskin cloak. He nodded to the painted clan boy who played the bone whistle. The boy blew harder, his face red, the sound so high and pointed it hurt Mothgirl's ears.

Vulture opened his arms wide, his bearskin stretched taut like wings, revealing the knife he wore around his neck as a pendant. Mothgirl gasped; it was the finest knife she had ever seen – carved from an antler, it was as long as her arm, white as a new moon, sharp as lynx claw. She longed for the knife – oh, the fine fine hunting she could do with an antler knife like that! Vulture tugged the knife and its tie gave way. He walked close close to Pa. He held the point to Pa's chest. The painful music stopped, with a sudden shriek.

'Behold!' hissed Vulture, quiet-voiced and dangerous.

Pa did not move. The fire shifted, shooting up sparks.

Vulture snatched Pa's hand and pressed the holding place of the knife into Pa's palm. 'Yours, oh Eagle! All yours!' His voice dripped like honey. 'Behold, Eagle, behold the great plenty!'

Pa held Vulture's gaze. Mothgirl held her breath.

Pa laid the antler knife upon the rock. At last he spoke. 'Yes, Vulture. I see these fine gifts. Yet you say you come to me with a bargain. I do not see what you ask of me in return.'

Vulture gave another nod to the red-faced flute boy who took a deep breath and lifted his bone whistle once more …

'No,' said Pa. 'No music. Enough!'

'*Pooooop!*' went the boy's bone whistle as, in his

surprise, he sucked air into it by mistake. Mothgirl giggled, in spite of herself, and she saw a giggle sparkle in the painted boy's eyes too.

Vulture's eyes, on the other hand, flashed only with menace. 'Very well,' he murmured. 'Very well, Eagle. You behold how Vulture is kind. You behold how kind, kind Vulture brings the great, great plenty. It is much, Eagle! Perhaps … too much … perhaps Vulture is too kind … perhaps …'

'Speak plain, Vulture. What is it you want from me?'

Vulture closed his eyes. Opened them again. And for the first time, he smiled; his teeth were sharpened to fine white points.

He whispered, but Mothgirl heard his hissed words.

'Vulture wants your daughter, Eagle. Vulture wants your daughter.'

NOT A GOOD IDEA

The wolf howled again.

Dara ran faster, bare feet slapping on the hard, wet sand. In his brain, Dara knew running was *not a good idea*; he knew that a wolf was not possible. But his ears heard what they heard and, in the dizzy frenzy of fear, his arms and legs and muscles just did what they did.

Rain stung his cheeks and his heart beat like thunder and wind whistled, high and flute-ish in his ears. For a tiny minute, Dara's fear melted with the astonishment of his own quickness – he felt electric blue like an eel in dark water, fast and free and wildly alive. Fearless. Wolf-proof. Like he could run and run on this huge beach forever.

His fear cracked like an eggshell and fell from him in fragments; he laughed aloud, a strange mad cackle; he didn't even sound like himself.

Then his laugh became choked, tangled, a cough. His

feet got heavier. Slowed and stopped. Dara wasn't running any more.

He was bent double, panting. He closed his eyes as his heart stampeded in the rhythm of a hundred galloping hooves.

Dara felt his legs go all loose like cooked spaghetti, crumpling under his weight. The sand was sugar-soft, Dara noticed, as he fell to his knees.

The whole grey world was spinning, like he was stuck in a whirling machine full of pencil-drawn candyfloss. Dara felt the tilt of it. He was losing his balance; he tried to put his arms out to save himself, but his arms were spaghetti too. Very, very slowly Dara saw the pale sand rush towards him. He closed his eyes and mouth and heard the soft thud-crunch of his own face landing. Then, seconds later, he felt the damp grainy coolness on his cheek.

In his brain, he knew he should move. Get up. Find his puffer. Get help. But his body wasn't listening. Like it had lost its signal. He couldn't even lift his hand to wipe the sand out of his eyes.

Daaaaaraaaaa!

A noise, far off. A howl? The wolf?

Daaaaraaaaaa!

Or was it … a voice?

Daaaaaraaaaaa!

Yes … a voice. Calling his name?

Dara squinted through his sand-dusted eyes, getting his bearings. He was lying in a little hollow by a gorse bush, right at the foot of the dunes.

Daaaaraaaaaa!

Dad?

He took a big shaky breath. He could feel his heart-beat steadying, catching up with itself again.

He wriggled his fingers.

He wriggled his toes.

He spat sand from his mouth.

He was … OK …

Was he … OK?

Daaaaraaaaaa!

Dad! Definitely Dad.

Dara opened his mouth to call back, but suddenly he snapped it shut. Dad couldn't find him like this! He'd know he'd been running; he'd be in heaps of trouble. Dara could almost imagine Dad's voice already: disap-pointed, cross, worried all at once: *You've taken it one step too far, Dara.*

Carefully, Dara pushed himself to sitting, very, very slowly like he was as delicate and fragile as a boy spun from glass. Dad would never believe that Dara was try-ing to run away from a wolf.

'A wolf?' whispered Dara, his voice so husky he

sounded like a cartoon baddie. Suddenly Dara wondered if *he* believed himself. What wolf?

Dara peered along the long, long beach. Only a distant dog walker in a yellow jacket and far off on the jetty by the Old Boatshed, a fisherman stood, just a grey silhouette, almost blended in to the waves and the drizzle.

There was no stupid wolf. What had he been thinking?

With shaky hands he unzipped his bag and took his puffer from its pocket. He breathed. He was fine. He was fine. Dara took another puff. He was fine.

'Daaaaaraaaa!' Dad's voice was close now.

Dara staggered to his feet. Trying to look casual, he brushed the sand from his face with his T-shirt but his T-shirt was sandy too. He squinted up to the top of the sand dune just as Dad's head popped over its crest – Dad looked like a little lost meerkat. From nowhere, Dara started to giggle. But his giggle turned into a snort, into a breathless wheezy bent-double cough.

'Daaaraaaa!' Dad came charging down the dune towards Dara, clouds of sand rising up behind him. 'Dara! You're pale as a mushroom. I saw you running like your life depended on it. What happened out there? Are you all right?'

Dara couldn't hide it. He couldn't pretend. He couldn't even speak.

'Oh, Dara, love.' Dad put his arm around him.

Somehow the warm comfort of it made Dara start to cry. Gulping, breathless sobs.

'Oh, love,' said Dad again, his eyes full of kindness and pity. 'Let's get you home.'

Dara felt little. Little and pathetic. He rubbed angrily at his eyes with scratchy, sandy fingers.

He wanted to wriggle out of Dad's hug. He wanted to say, 'No thanks, Dad. I'll get *myself* home. I don't need *your* help.' But he still couldn't speak. And he couldn't walk properly either. His legs were still all wobbly.

Reluctant and angry and sad, Dara leaned on Dad and Dad half carried him really as, slowly, slowly, they made their way through the dunes towards the cottage.

SECRET

When he woke up, Dara felt a tightness across his cheeks, strangely familiar, like a memory, like an old friend. His eyes flickered open and he remembered that he was wearing *Darth*, his oxygen mask; he hadn't had to wear Darth since last winter. Dara rubbed his eyes and glanced out of the window; he couldn't tell how long he'd been asleep, but it was still only afternoon. Dara lay back and breathed Darth's air, it tasted cooler and bluer and fuller than ordinary air.

Dara listened. They were arguing downstairs, Mum and Dad. The edges of their voices poked through the whirring hum of Dara's oxygen machine, like spiky feathers through a pillow. He couldn't hear the words but he knew they were arguing about him; he knew it was his fault.

Years ago, when he was eight or nine even, it would've

been fine – to run like that, just for a minute or two. But not any more. Now he needed to walk everywhere ploddishly just like Nero, the old dog who lived next door, back at Mandel. Sometimes Margot let Dara take Nero for a walk in the forest after school; they had to stick to the top path though because Nero had a bad hip so he struggled with steps now. Dara smiled bitterly; he struggled with steps too, to be honest. *Like an old grey-whiskered dog!* he thought to himself glumly.

Then he gave himself a shake. It'd all be different soon though; after the Big Op he'd be bouncing everywhere like a puppy!

Tap-tap-tap. Mum knocked ever so lightly on his door with just her nails.

Dara lifted Darth and breathed the real air; it tasted thin, like too-weak squash. 'I'm awake!' he said, slipping in his nose tubes. 'Come in!'

The door opened slowly; Mum came in and sat on his bed. Dad sat under the eaves, on the bed that used to be Charlie's back when Charlie was younger and still came on family holidays. Mum checked Dara's oxygen levels. 'Surprisingly fine,' she said, with a weak little smile.

'Sorry, Mum. Sorry, Dad,' said Dara, voice still croaky. He looked down, traced his finger along the paths of the checked pattern on the duvet. 'It was a stupid thing to do.'

Mum was probably thinking, *Yes, utterly stupid, Dara, you total nitwit*, but she didn't say it. She just rubbed his arm and did that strange sad smile again. He'd kind of rather she simply told him off and got it over with.

But she didn't tell him off. She didn't say anything. Neither did Dad.

The room was so quiet that Dara heard a gull land on the roof, walk a few scrabbly steps, then take off again. He looked out the window, following the gull's flight with his eyes as she glided off through the grey sky towards Lathrin Island.

Dad followed his gaze. 'We were thinking of maybe taking you there tomorrow,' he said. 'See if we can find that golden rabbit.' He gave Dara a little wink, like he always did when he made that daft joke.

'Golden *Hare*, Dad!' corrected Dara, like he always did too.

Dad smiled, but his smile wasn't right; it was all watery like Mum's. Hang on. Mum and Dad knew perfectly well he had his heart set on going to Lathrin Island all by himself after the Big Op. They knew about his plan. Why were they suddenly saying *they'd* bring him out there? Dara looked from Dad to Mum and back again. Something was wrong.

'Mum, Dad, I don't know what to say. I'm really, really sorry,' said Dara, throwing his arms in the air. 'I just got

32

it wrong. I know it was *not a good idea*. I usually stick to everything you say and everything Dr Da Silva says and I know what to do and what not to do but for some reason I just – I just didn't.'

'Dara, love. Stop. Calm down.' Mum was looking anxiously at the numbers on the machine screen. 'We're not cross, love. We're just ...' She glanced at Dad out of the corner of her eye.

Dad was biting his lip. Like how he did when he was trying really hard not to say something. Something secret.

'What is it?' said Dara quietly.

Mum and Dad looked at each other. A complicated look that Dara didn't understand. Mum was biting her lip now too; Dara could see tears swimming in her eyes.

'Mum?' he gasped. Mum didn't cry!

'We weren't going to tell you. Not yet. We didn't want to spoil ...' Mum's voice was all squeaky.

'... we didn't want to spoil your holiday.' Dad came over and sat on Dara's bed too. He put his arm around Mum and reached for Dara's hand.

'What's going to spoil my holiday?' whispered Dara, his voice moth-quiet.

Suddenly Dara realised. 'No ...' he whispered quietly under his breath.

TROUBLE GIRL

In the dark of the hut Mothgirl's heart clenched. Vulture's words clasped her tight. 'No!' she gasped. Airless with shock. Like a fish ripped from the water by an eagle's beak.

'*Vulture wants your daughter.*'

She could not breathe. 'NO!' she yelled, bursting out from her hiding place in the hut. 'NO! You NOT take me, Vulture! NO!'

Vulture; the bone-flute boy; the painted clansmen; Owlboy in his hiding place; Pa by the fireside: they all stared at her, open-mouthed.

Standing there with all these eyes upon her, Mothgirl felt suddenly small and weak and alone, like that young deer down by the riverbank. 'No!' Mothgirl said again, but this time her voice trembled.

'*ACCK-ACCK-ACCK-AACCCCCK!*' It was Vulture;

he was bent double. *'ACCK-ACCK-ACCK-AACCCCK!'* What was wrong? Was he choking? Pa leaned towards him with a steadying hand.

But Vulture straightened. *'ACCK-ACCK-ACCK.'* His lips were drawn back, showing his sharpened teeth, and Mothgirl realised that he was not choking; he was laughing.

All around the camp, Vulture's men began laughing too, thin imitations of their leader's crow-voiced cackle. *'Ack-ack,'* they chortled, nudging one another. *'Ack-ack-ack.'*

Their fools' laughter prickled Mothgirl, made her feel hot with anger and cold with shame. 'Why you laugh?' she said.

The men laughed more loudly, all but the bone-flute boy, who just stared silently at the ground and twisted at his deertooth necklace with his painted fingers. And Vulture, Vulture laughed louder than them all. *'ACCK-ACCK-ACCK!'*

Mothgirl looked desperately to Pa. Pa was not laughing. He was solemn-eyed. He beckoned her to him and Mothgirl stood by Pa's side. Although she could feel how her knees shook with rage and shame and fear, she held her face rock-firm and stone-steady. Pa raised his hand, palm open, asking silence, in the way it was done.

One by one, Vulture's men ceased their noise, until only Vulture's laugh remained. He shook his head, sighing, like all this mirth had made him weary. 'Ahh, Eagle, the girl gives you much trouble, I see! Vulture will take your trouble. Kind Vulture will mend the ways of this trouble girl. *NO!* she speaks. To her own good father. *NO*, indeed! She will quick learn – the girls of Vulture's clan do not speak *NO!*' His cold eyes pierced Mothgirl's, sharp as a speartip.

She looked quick away, straight-staring beyond him to where the evening sky rippled red like fire, amber like tree sap, yellow like lynx eye. Up on the hilltop she saw shadow shapes that made her heart pang – there was Eelgirl crouched behind the Spirit Stone, and next to her stood ByMySide, ears alert, watchful and ready. She was deep glad her wolf knew to be wary and to keep away; not all men could be trusted.

'Vulture,' said Pa. 'I give thanks. Your gifts are good. But I ask you this: Why you want my daughter; why you want my Mothgirl? She is but twelve summers old. She is young, Vulture. She is too young to leave our clan.'

Mothgirl felt relief pour through her like nectar. Then, to her surprise, Vulture laughed, this time louder than ever. His men, of course, joined with his laughter. She saw Pa's brow furrow slightly.

'Why you laugh, Vulture?'

'*ACCK-ACCK!* Ah, Eagle! Ah, I laugh! That a good

36

question indeed, Eagle. *Why* Vulture want this girl?'
Vulture pointed a painted finger at Mothgirl. Mothgirl
winced. 'This girl. Your daughter. This girl is trouble
girl. Look her!'

Mothgirl felt the sharp pinch of all eyes upon her
once more; she watched her feet and wished herself
small as a pebble.

'Look this girl! Look her man spear! Look her man
deerskin! This girl not know woman ways, she know
man ways! This girl hunt, Eagle! This girl speak "No!"
Eagle, hear me. It is not the way!'

Mothgirl saw Pa's fist tighten. *Some things are done
and some things are simply not the way.* That was what Pa
himself always said. She winced, knowing how much
Pa hated not doing things the way they ought be done.

'Now, listen, Eagle; Vulture need to tell you some
hard truth. Vulture knows your son is gone. Hart is
gone now. Vulture saw Hart's waymarker out beyond
the Great Plain. Hart is gone, Eagle. It is a hard truth.'

NO! screamed Mothgirl's mind-voice, but she did not
let it out. She saw the muscle line in Pa's neck tighten
like a pulled vine.

Vulture's words oozed on, smooth and sweet as
honey. 'Vulture comes in kindness. Vulture want help
you, Eagle. Vulture will help you find dear lost Hart.
Vulture will bring your son to you.'

'*Ack-ack-ack,*' came the quiet, under-breath laughter of Vulture's men.

Vulture came close now, like a spider with a fly in his sticky web. 'Oh, Eagle, how it pains Vulture to speak hard truth to you, but all the clans ... they laugh at you, Eagle. All the clans they laugh at you and they laugh at your daughter. They tell of your daughter in their fire-stories. *Ha!* they tell. *Ha! Eagle's girl is half girl, half wolf! Ha!* they tell. *Eagle's girl hunt like man. Ha!* they tell, *Eagle's girl grow a big fine beard one day!*'

'*Ack-ack-ack,*' laughed one of Vulture's men. Vulture's eyes proudened.

Mothgirl felt sickness swirl in her belly; she squeezed back the tears that prickled in her eyes. *Untrue! Untrue!* she longed to shout, but she dared not, for fear of shaming Pa, for fear of being the *trouble girl* cruel Vulture spoke of. If Hart was here Hart would have shouted the words she longed to yell. Hart would have chased Vulture from here with one wave of his proud spear. 'Speak on,' said Pa. His voice heavy. 'I listen.'

Mothgirl's stomach lurched. She could not bear to hear more.

'Good, Eagle. Good,' said Vulture, honey-voiced. 'Vulture speak with full kindness. Vulture come here to help you. Eagle, it is not yet too late! Your daughter, she is still young enough to learn. Vulture will take this trouble girl from you and Vulture will tame her.'

Mothgirl winced.

Vulture flashed his sharpened teeth, scooping a handful of clay from the ground. 'Daughters are clay, Eagle. We shape them how *we* choose – that is the way. Vulture will take your trouble girl and –' he squeezed the clay hard between his hands, pinching and prodding and rolling roughly – 'Vulture will shape your trouble girl until she learns better ways, until all trouble gone.' He held up a tight ball of clay, round as a dropping. 'And when she is good, I will give your daughter to my son.'

For a tiny second Pa and Mothgirl's eyes met, a spinning, confused look.

'Your son?' said Pa.

VOLEBOY

'Come, Vole, show yourself!' said Vulture, gesturing impatiently with his spear.

The bone-flute boy shuffled forward, his eyes low. He stood next to his father.

'Behold Vole, son of great Vulture, son of proud Lynx of the Sky Plains!' bellowed Vulture. 'Behold!'

Mothgirl beheld. She beheld how Vole was a head smaller than she was. She beheld how his spear hand trembled and how his throat apple was not yet grown. *Vole?* she thought to herself. *This not Vole; this Voleboy!*

Pa clearly had the same thinkings. 'Your son, Vulture,' said Pa slowly, almost kindly. 'Your son is young, is he not? Too young also perhaps?'

Mothgirl saw Vulture's eyes darken in the depths of his blood-paint mask. All laughter gone. 'You think I know not my own son, Eagle?' He spat on the ground and turned to the boy. 'Vole! Speak me – how many summers you have?'

The boy's eyes remained low. 'Twelve summers,' he mumbled.

Vulture pressed the point of his spear to his son's throat. 'You man? You Vole?'

'Yes! Yes! I man. I Vole.' The boy's voice squeaked in terror.

Vulture lowered his spear and nodded solemnly. 'Man!' he declared.

Mothgirl narrowed her eyes and stared at the boy: how pale his face was beneath the streaks of blood paint; how thin his arms; how trembling his hands. Voleboy. Not *Vole*. Of that she was certain. And she pitied him.

The boy's frightened eyes flicked up and met hers. She shot him a look of venom and lightning. Swift, he looked back at the ground.

She pitied this boy, but she did not want to be his. She did not want to be anybody's.

Mothgirl held her chin proudly in the air as Voleboy backed away from the fireside and into the shadows. *Ha!* she thought to herself, and she turned back to Pa, not noticing the boy who had slid silently into the forest.

'What say you, oh Eagle?' hissed Vulture.

Pa rubbed his chin and stared into the fire.

Mothgirl held her breath. She closed her eyes and wished, from her toes to her hair roots, that Hart would come home right at that very moment; she imagined Hart laughing in the face of foolish Voleboy and spitting in the face of cruel Vulture and throwing sand in the faces of all the blood-stink, untrue, painted men. Hart did not care, like Pa did, for the old ways, for doing what should be done. Oh, Hart!

But Hart did not come. She opened her eyes and stared up at the first stars.

'Speak, Eagle,' said Vulture, his voice twisted and snake-like. 'What say you?'

Pa was silent. He did not look at Mothgirl. He did not look at Vulture. He stared into the fire like his mind was heavy with thoughts.

Mothgirl watched, dry-tongued, as Pa held *yes* in one hand and *no* in the other hand, and weighed each against the other. She bit her lip. 'What say you, Pa?' she whispered under her breath.

Pa lifted his eyes from the flames. He cleared his throat, preparing to speak.

NEWS

Dad cleared his throat, preparing to speak.

But Dara could feel the news already. Heavy as a storm cloud in the bedroom air.

'While you were asleep, we called the hospital and spoke to Dr Da Silva,' said Mum.

'We explained to her what happened today, down on the beach,' said Dad.

The rain pattered on the windowpane. Dara sighed. He knew what was coming. He hadn't had a really bad episode like this in years, not since that time when he was ten at Nisha Caro's party; Dara cringed at the memory of waking up lying on the trampoline with everyone from school peering in through the netting at him, like he was a creature in a zoo. Trampolines were *not a good idea*.

Dara bit his lip. 'We have to go to the hospital, don't

we?' he said. 'I've got to go in for tests. I'm so sorry. I've ruined our holid—'

'No, love,' said Dad, with that watery weak smile. 'No, love, our holiday's fine. You don't have to go to hospital. It's …'

Dad looked at Mum. Mum looked at Dad. They both looked at Dara.

'It's the Big Op,' said Mum. 'Dr Da Silva thinks that it's not a good idea.'

'Not just yet – '

'Maybe in a month or two – '

'Best let everything settle back down again – '

'And then – '

'We'll see – '

Their voices faded away, like words underwater. Dara closed his eyes. Tight. Like knots. He squeezed his fingers to fists and curled up his toes under the duvet and inside himself he clasped every single muscle he could reach.

But still the tears got out. He could taste them, salty as seawater, on his bitten-tight lips.

'Oh, Dara,' said Mum. And she was cuddling him. And Dad was cuddling him too.

But he didn't cuddle them back, he wanted to push them away. He wanted to burst out of their cuddle like a firework and soar up into the rain-dark sky and explode like dragon breath into firedust and sparks and roaring screaming fury.

But he didn't burst. He curled everything tighter, shrinking himself away.

Around him Mum talked and Dad talked. Their words fell like leaves. Like snowflakes. Like blossom. Dara didn't even try to catch them. Because he knew it would be pointless. All that mattered was what he knew already.

The Big Op wasn't going to happen.

Two weeks tomorrow. The day he'd circled in gold on the calendar, brighter than his birthday, brighter than Christmas. The day that had been so fixed and so bright and so certain, the day that would change everything. It would just be an ordinary day. On that day *nothing* was going to happen.

And perhaps nothing was ever going to change. Maybe *this* was all there was, all *he* was, all he'd ever be.

The beep of the oxygen machine cut through the underwater rise and fall of Mum's and Dad's voices. Automatically, Dara flicked the switch and took out his nose tubes.

He'd stopped crying. He felt cold and still as ice.

'Dara?' said Mum, softly.

Dara blinked at her for a second. 'Sorry? What did you say?'

'Here, take these.' She was holding a pharmacy packet towards him. 'Dr Da Silva sent through an emergency prescription; Dad went to pick them up from the chemist while you were sleeping. You're to take one at bedtime and one in the morning.'

Blearily Dara opened the box. Pink tablets. More stupid medicine to take. 'What do these ones do?' he said flatly.

Mum squeezed his hand. 'They're new ones, strong ones. They should prevent any reactions like you had today.'

'The Pink Pills of Power!' said Dad, flexing his pretend muscles. Trying to be funny.

Dara rolled his eyes; he wasn't in the mood for funny. 'I'm tired,' he said. His voice felt empty like he was a robot, made of metal. He slid down under the covers and closed his eyes, pulling the duvet around his ears.

Mum's and Dad's voices came and went around him, until he felt the softness of their kisses on his hair and heard Dad whisper 'See you in the morning, son-shine' like he always did. Then the gentle click of the door closing behind them.

And Dara was alone.

He reached over the side of the bed and pulled up his backpack; unzipping the pocket, he took out his brass hare. Dara stared at the hare just sitting there on the palm of his hand; heavy and gleaming, watchful and waiting, ears alert, paws ready.

Totally and utterly useless, just a lump of stupid metal too. There was no such thing as luck.

Dara shoved the pointless, ridiculous hare back in his bag and he buried his face in his soft pillow and he opened his mouth and he screamed, silently at the top of his voice, for minutes and minutes until his throat was raw.

CHOICE

Mothgirl wanted to scream, to bite, to fight, to run. She did not dare look at Vulture. She did not dare look at Pa. She stared into the leaping flames of the fire that crackled and sparked. In the darkening forest a hunted creature shrieked. Mothgirl squeezed her fists so tight she felt her bones would crack. She knew that nothing she could do would make any difference. She had no choice. No power. She was caught like a hare in a trap.

Mothgirl stared at the heap of promises piled up by the fireside – the deerskins, the arrowheads, the fish, the knife, the teeth, the boar. *The great plenty.* She looked down at her own self – her mud-caked feet; her strong legs; her rabbit-skin cape; her tatty deerskin; her well-worn spear. Was this all she was? Was this all she ever had been? Just another promise to be traded for the highest price when the time was right; as precious and powerless as a dead, bloody boar?

Pa cleared his throat again. He raised his open palm. And finally he spoke.

'Vulture. Be patient. I will speak awhile with my daughter.'

Mothgirl felt her knees buckle with relief. She gripped Pa's shoulder to steady herself.

Vulture laughed his cruel laugh. 'He will *speak with his daughter*!' he repeated mockingly to his men. They laughed too. Then Vulture turned back to Pa, his eyes glinting, and pointed to the rising moon. 'Speak fast, Eagle. Vulture is kind. But Vulture does not like to wait – when moon is high, Vulture goes,' he whispered. 'With trouble girl, or without trouble girl.' He spat into the fire, which hissed like a warning.

Pa nodded and rose to his feet, awkward and massive like a great bear. He lumbered into the dark of the forest edge and Mothgirl followed, her unspilt tears held tight in her belly.

As she passed Vulture he reached out fast and grabbed her arm. Mothgirl gasped; his fingers were tight as teeth. Heart thudding, she turned and stared defiantly into his moon-yellow eyes, breathing the ripe stench of his blood paint.

'Trouble girl,' he said, his voice dangerously soft and purrish. 'Do not fight Vulture, trouble girl! You. Will. Lose.' Quick as a snake tongue he dipped his finger into the pool of blackening boar blood and drew a line with it along Mothgirl's cheek.

Mothgirl cried out. She wriggled from his grip and stumbled away after Pa, rubbing at her bloodied face with her arm. She tried not to hear the *ACK-ACK-ACK* of Vulture's laughter coming at her through the shadows like a cloud of bats.

'Pa,' she whispered, her voice full of trembles. 'Where you?'

'I here,' said Pa, sitting on a rock in the dark. He sounded weary.

She went to him and sat at his feet. He put his hand on her head and softly stroked her hair. 'Mothgirl, my girl,' he said. 'You not have woman ways. You not have man ways. You have Mothgirl ways. But Mothgirl. Hear me: winter comes. I am old. I am not strong. I am not fast. I cannot make you safe.'

'But Hart ...'

'Hart is gone.'

Hearing his big voice tremble, she wrapped her arms around Pa's knees and let the tears fall free down her blood-smeared cheeks. 'No, Pa,' she said, squeak-voiced.

Pa's words were whispers now. 'Go with Vulture, Mothgirl. Go.'

'No, Pa. No!' sobbed Mothgirl, clinging to him. 'No, Pa! I cannot. No. Vulture want to shape me like clay, Pa!'

'Hear me, my Mothgirl.' He held her face in his hands, wiping her tears softly with his big rough fingers. 'You twelve summers old! You need learn woman ways – it is time!'

'I know woman ways – Mole taught me woman ways, Pa!'

'No, Mothgirl, not enough. Dear Mole is in spirit sleep. Listen me; I not want that *great plenty* Vulture bring here. I not want fine deerskins. I not want picture-spears.'

Hope flickered in Mothgirl's heart. She blinked up at Pa.

Pa kissed her head. 'I want make safe my Mothgirl,' he whispered. 'Vulture is strong man. Vulture have many strong men. Vole is good man for you.'

Mothgirl threw her hands in the air, anger bursting through her tears. 'Vole *not* man! Vole *boy*! Vole not strong man! Vulture not strong man! Vulture not wise man! Vulture stinking painted shadow man! Vulture untrue! Untrue!'

'Enough, Mothgirl!' said Pa, his voice gruff now. 'Some things are done. And some things are simply not

51

the way. You are my daughter; I am your father. I speak; you listen. I say go; you go.'

'Pa!' Her breath came in short hiccuping rasps. 'I am your daughter, Pa. I am your Mothgirl. No, Pa! No!' She clasped his knees with all her strength and she could feel his sobs come trembling then too, like earthshakes.

'Go with Vulture!' said Pa's choked voice. 'Go, my Mothgirl.'

Some things are done. And some things are simply not the way.

She had no choice. Mothgirl staggered to her feet, wiping tears from her cheeks.

'Good girl,' whispered Pa. 'It is right. It is how it must be.'

But Mothgirl could not look at him. With wobbly legs and low eyes she stumbled towards the clearing and the *ack-ack* laughter and the flickering firelight.

Just on the edge of the shadows she paused. High on the moonlit hilltop ByMySide was watching her. He howled. A call so wild and lonely.

Aching with broken love, Mothgirl lifted her chin to the moon and howled her very own wild, lonely cry.

Go with Vulture's clan? How could this be the way?

Mothgirl tightened her spear hand. Then she turned and she ran, lynx-fast, into the dark of the night forest. And away.

RIVER

Alone. Free. Afraid.

Mothgirl ran fast through the dark like the forest floor was on fire, her toes barely touched the ground she moved so quick, more like flying than running. She did not keep to the track; that would be foolish; Vulture and his men would find her easily that way. Instead she charged headlong through the twisted undergrowth: the sharp rip of her skin on thorns, the tear of her hair on tangled twigs, the thud and the scamper and the leap of her fast fast feet.

Behind her Mothgirl could hear shouts. Cruel laughter. Breaking branches. A hunt. She ran faster.

Down the hill Mothgirl ran, skidding, slipping, righting herself. She didn't pause at the river for even a breath, she ran right into the cold black water, until, when she was neck-deep, the force of the current knocked her off balance.

She heard Vulture's mocking *accck-accck* laugh close by as she slid away, gasping a last mouthful of air, before the river closed over her head.

Mothgirl spun around and around in the whirling black water, so that moon was down and riverbed was up, and the fast current swirled her and whooshed her downstream. To where there were rocks, smooth and dark as sleeping whales.

Mothgirl didn't see it looming. Deep underwater her head cronked silently on to the rock. Darkest dark.

Her body loosened. Drifted. Soft and bending like a willow frond.

The river slowed, carried Mothgirl gently to the quiet place, where white moon rippled in still black water. And there the river left her body, floating and still in the pearly light.

CAVE

Mothgirl felt her body gently lifted from the river and laid on cold rock.

Was she in spirit sleep? Were her waking days ended?

Her belly up-squeezed. Water, so much water, poured from her mouth, her nose, her eyes. She gasped a breath. Coughed. And another breath.

Lying there, eyes closed, her head thumped dizzily. She felt a sharp nip on her earlobe; a stinging pinch that zinged with living. Her heart soared with relief; she was not in spirit sleep! She was in her waking days still!

Something warm and rough stroked her cheek and her hair over and over. She smelt a smell she knew. A smell like forest and meat and rain. ByMySide!

Mothgirl felt the quick nip of his teeth on her ear again. She opened her eyes and flung her arms around the wolf's neck, burying her face in his damp fur. He shook her off gently and carried on licking her dry. She lay exhausted, shivering in this darkest dark.

'Where this place?' she said, and her quiet voice echoed. 'Where am me?'

'Shhhhhhhh!' hissed a voice from the deeper dark.

Someone else was here. ByMySide growled softly and fear danced with ice feet on Mothgirl's skin.

She could see nothing but she heard drips dropping and the air smelt wet-cold. She was in a cave.

But who else was in this cave with her?

Then Mothgirl heard other voices; man voices. She looked towards the voices and saw a jagged crack of pale moonlight where the cave opening must be. Mothgirl held her breath and listened as the man voices came closer.

'Where she?' spoke a gruff man voice.

'I not know where she, Viper!' the other replied. 'Trouble girl tracks stop at river.'

'Maybe not trouble girl! Maybe trouble fish!'

Ack-ack-ack!'

The shadow shapes of Vulture's men blocked the thin band of moonlight. Their footsteps stopped stepping. Mothgirl heard a loud sniff.

'You smell wolf stench?' whispered one of the man voices.

Terror clasped Mothgirl's pounding heart; she dug her fingers deeper into ByMySide's fur.

The other man voice sniffed. 'Ha! *You* make wolf stench!' he answered, his *ack-ack* laugh echoing eerily in the dark as the men walked away.

Slowly Mothgirl breathed again.

The voice in the deeper cave-dark breathed too.

'Hart?' whispered Mothgirl. 'That you there, Hart?'

No answer. No Hart.

'Who you?' said Mothgirl.

Vulture? said Mothgirl's fearful thinkings. *Vulture had trapped her here …*

Mothgirl's spear was gone. She reached into her pouch, and from amongst the wet hawthorn leaves she drew her skinning blade, and held it in her fist. 'Who you? Show you!' she hissed as she edged slowly into the dark.

A shuffle sound, scuffle sound.

Mothgirl turned. Where the moonlight crept in, a shadow shape was shoving and heaving on a rock; the rock rolled aside and dim grey light poured into the cave. Mothgirl gasped.

DANGER-BOY

Standing in the cave mouth was the small pale shape of the boy who had played the bone whistle. The boy who had slipped off into the night. Voleboy. Vulture's very own son.

Mothgirl tightened her grip on her skinning blade and pointed its glinting sharpness at Voleboy.

He held his spear out in front of him, but as he stepped backwards away from her, his foot slid suddenly on cave pebbles and Voleboy fell to the ground with a sharp yelp, his spear rolling out of his hand and into the shadows.

Mothgirl sprang. She crouched above the boy, her blade to his fast-rising chest. 'Why you take me?' she hissed. 'Why you put me in this dark dark cave?'

'I ... I ... I ...' he whimpered. She pressed her blade closer. 'I – I – I not take you. I find you! I make safe!'

Mothgirl rubbed her throbbing head, trying to remember: *The cold river. The dark. Could it be true?*

'You? *You* make safe *me?*' she murmured, and she drew back her blade away from the boy.

ByMySide growled, like a warning. But Mothgirl was not fast enough. Quick like a snake Voleboy was up, and on his feet. He seized something long and thin and white from his waist pouch.

Mothgirl remembered Vulture's antler knife. Sharp and deadly. Why had she listened? Why had she believed? *This boy not want make safe! This danger-boy!* She leaped back.

But ByMySide did not retreat with her. The brave wolf padded slowly *towards* Voleboy, making thunder-groans deep in his belly. The boy with the moon-white knife held his ground as the wolf sank low, preparing to pounce.

'No!' yelled Mothgirl. She would *not* let this danger boy kill ByMySide. She would not!

Mothgirl ran at the boy like an angry boar, head first and bellowing. She knocked him flat and they fell together to the ground, clawing and biting and tearing at each other as they rolled and kicked and spat.

Both on their knees now, eye to eye and panting, Mothgirl grabbed the boy's wrist and at the exact same moment Voleboy grabbed hers. They froze, teeth-gritted, locked together in fury. They each fire-stared deep into the other's burning eyes.

ByMySide made that strange sound again; the deep belly groan. Mothgirl gave him a side look. It was not a growl; it was not a danger noise; it was like the noise he had made back when he was pup-small and hungry; what was he telling her?

'Wolf want wolfsong,' said the boy, still breathing heavy. He spat.

Mothgirl heard the small *tink-tink* of a lost boy-tooth rolling on rock; she felt proud-hearted at her own fierce fight-strength.

'*Wolfsong?*' she said, mocking-voiced. 'What *wolfsong?*'

Voleboy grunted. 'You let go my arm; I show you wolfsong!'

'Ha!' said Mothgirl, tightening her grip. 'I let go your arm; you not show me *wolfsong* – you show me spirit sleep! I not foolish!'

The boy's lips twitched. 'I show you spirit sleep?! With *what* I show you spirit sleep? With *this*?' The boy let go a little laugh and waggled the long white blade.

Why he laugh at her? Mothgirl looked hard then, and in the dim grey moonlight she realised that what Voleboy held in his hand was not Vulture's death-sharp antler knife. No ...

'That ... that ... your bone whistle ...' she mumbled.

60

She stared, wide-eyed and astonished, at the long white flute.

The boy laughed so hard then that Mothgirl felt his laugh shake through his arms. He made a little gasp, then a big snort noise came from his nose.

Mothgirl's lips twitched then too. 'You sound like small boar,' she said, and she threw down his wrist.

Voleboy dropped her wrist too. He rubbed at the hurt place where she had held him. 'You fight like small *bear*!' he said.

They laughed together, then solemnly they made the sign of spirit peace with their open hands.

An owl hooted in the forest dark. Voleboy and Mothgirl leaned warily out of the cave mouth, listening for man voices.

There were none.

Mothgirl peered up at the hilltop, far upstream, where firelight faintly flickered. *Home. Pa.* Her heart ached.

She glanced at Voleboy; his eyes were fixed on her camp too. *Why?* she wondered. *Why had Voleboy not betrayed her to his clansmen when they came hunting? Why had he hidden with her here in this cave?* She stared hard at his face then, but even though his blood paint was gone, Mothgirl could read no answers there.

'Come,' said Voleboy quietly.

WOLFSONG

They climbed down to the river's edge and sat silently side by side on a rock in the moonlight, Mothgirl and Voleboy, wiping their own cuts clean with sting-leaf and water, listening to owl-hoot and river-splash.

ByMySide lay at their feet on the river sand, with his head on his paws, still making his strange rumble-belly-groan.

'What wolfsong?' said Mothgirl quietly.

'Listen,' said Voleboy. He took his bone whistle from his pouch and put it to his lips.

ByMySide's ears pricked. He raised his big grey head, looking all around.

'I not hear wolfsong!' whispered Mothgirl.

'Shhhhh!' said Voleboy with a small smile. 'You girl! Girl not hear wolfsong; wolf hear wolfsong!' He took another breath and he blew again.

Mothgirl watched, eyes wide, as ByMySide whimpered and whined, then rolled on to his back, pawing the air like he was a small wolf pup. She rubbed his furry belly in astonishment.

'Wolfsong!' said Voleboy, lowering his bone whistle.

Mothgirl blinked at him. 'Wolfsong!' she said admiringly. She held out her hand for the bone whistle. 'I try?'

Voleboy hesitated for a blink, then passed it to her.

Mothgirl put it to her lips and blew. Out came a noise like Pa's stink-wind. They both giggled.

She handed the bone whistle back to Voleboy. 'You play good wolfsong!' she said.

Voleboy shrugged.

The first whispers of morning were starting to pale the edges of the sky. Mothgirl knew she needed to go; she needed to find Hart; only Hart could help her. The journey towards the Great Plains would be safer now in the half-dark than later when the sun was full-bright.

She stood; ByMySide stood too. 'I go.'

'I come with you?' he asked quietly.

Mothgirl thought a moment, then shook her head, kind but firm. Friendship was a strange new taste to her, and she did not trust it. She would be swifter, stronger, better alone.

'Voleboy,' she said. He did not correct her. 'Voleboy, I give thanks.' Her voice was solemn; this boy had saved her from spirit sleep; this boy had saved her from Vulture's men. She wished she had a gift to give him as a sign of her thanks. She rummaged in her pouch, but all there was in there was her skinning blade, the hawthorn leaves, and …

Mothgirl pulled out the smooth flat pebble she'd slipped into her pouch earlier when she was playing jump-stones with Eelgirl and Owlboy. She pressed it into Voleboy's hand.

He turned it over in his fingers, his eyebrows low and puzzled. 'A stone?' he said. Mothgirl snatched back the pebble; an idea sparked in her.

With her skinning blade, Mothgirl scratched four lines on to the smooth jump-stone, carving the shape of open wings. It was a pattern she had scratched many times over, but only in hidden places – high on a tree trunk, deep in a cave – for it was the shape of Mothgirl's very own secret waymarker and she knew that girls ought not mark their way as men did.

'This not a stone,' she said. 'This a promise.' She passed the promise to Voleboy. 'You make-safe me, Voleboy. I give thanks. One day …' She closed his fingers around the pebble. 'One day I will see you again, Voleboy, and *I* will make-safe *you*.'

With her fingertip she drew an invisible circle on the back of Voleboy's hand. 'Make safe,' she whispered, and she let his hand fall. Mothgirl could not tell if he had even understood her promise, for he turned and scrambled back up to the cave without a word.

Mothgirl watched him go. She sighed, strangely sorrowful. Then, with ByMySide at her heel, she set off along the edge of the moonlit river, towards Hart and the hunting grounds at the Great Plain and – she shuddered – Lathrin Mountain beyond …

'Stop!'

Mothgirl turned around. Voleboy scrambled across the rocks after her.

'Here,' he said, and he handed her his spear.

She shook her head at his stupidity. 'I cannot take your spear, Voleboy! How you hunt? What you do when a real bear comes?! No, Voleboy. You foolish. Keep your spear.'

'I not need my spear, Mothgirl,' said Voleboy, and he waggled his bone whistle at her.

Mothgirl blinked; she did not understand.

'Wolfsong; bearsong; lynxsong; boarsong,' he said. 'I have spear because …' He shrugged. 'Because *man have spear*, it is *simply the way*. But, Mothgirl, I not need my spear to hunt. I not need my spear to make safe. I need my bone whistle.'

Voleboy offered her his spear again, and this time Mothgirl took it. 'I give thanks, Voleboy,' she said. 'I give big big thanks.'

65

Voleboy rubbed between ByMySide's ears, in the place the wolf loved best. 'I give thanks you, Mothgirl.' He smiled, wide and warm-hearted. 'One day, I will give that promise stone big big thanks!'

She smiled back at him, then she turned and, spear in hand, Mothgirl and her wolf disappeared into the night forest.

TRUE LEGENDS

Dara lifted his tear-blotched face from his pillow. To his surprise it was still day outside. The rain had stopped, and long low beams of sunshine reached into his room like golden fingers on an outstretched hand.

He sighed a shaky sigh and knelt on his bed, his elbows on his window sill. Out at sea Lathrin Island glowed gorse-yellow and impossible, mocking him almost with its brightness. The sea had changed colour now as well; it was like another sea entirely – placid and pale as a painting. A small white fishing boat crossed the strait; Dara watched it shrink and shrink as it ploughed straight through the water between the buoys that marked the safe route from the big harbour on the mainland to the small harbour out on Lathrin. By the time the boat had reached the island it was small as a bath toy. Dara watched it change course at Owl Rock before skirting the island's tip and disappearing out into the wild open ocean beyond. Owl Rock was named for a story about the owl who waited for so long on the headland she turned to actual stone; with a bitter little laugh he imagined himself as Dara-shaped rock; waiting, waiting, waiting …

He sighed again. He'd always loved all those legends about Lathrin Island; Charlie had read them to him so many times when he was little that Dara had known the stories pretty much off by heart even before he learned to read them for himself. Dara lifted the book from his window sill, its cover worn soft and its corners all raggedy; he ran his fingers over the once sparkly stars and the worn-out swirls of silver writing on the cover: *The True Legends of Lathrin Island*. He shivered, remembering that funny tingly dreamy feeling he'd always had when he was a little boy that one day he'd be part of these stories too; that he'd go to Lathrin and do something brave and heroic and legendary. Dara bit his lip.

Sinking back into his pillow, Dara opened the book for about the millionth time and he read.

The Golden Hare

Once, long long ago, when all our world was new, a hare was born. The other hares didn't quite know what to make

68

of her because this hare wasn't at all like they were: she wasn't brown or grey or black. The new hare was different; she had fur of pure gold and eyes of blue.

'She's surely bewitched,' whispered the other hares. 'She'll bring us ill luck.'

The golden hare's mother and the golden hare's father paid them no heed. 'A hare is a hare,' they said, and they raised her just the same as all their other young leverets.

But as the golden hare grew long-eared and tall, she found it harder and harder to ignore the sharp looks and whispers as she passed. Each morning she wished she would wake at dusk with brown eyes and brown fur, invisible like that, one of many. But alas it was not to be, for the golden hare grew more golden by the day, and also more lonely.

One terrible winter a sickness came amongst the hares. One by one their ears drooped and their eyes closed, never to reopen.

'We told you that golden hare would bring ill luck,' said the other hares. 'She must leave before her witching sickness catches every last one of us.'

So one full-moon night they drove the golden hare out across the frozen fields all the way to the sea. 'Go!' they cried, forcing her into the icy water. 'Swim away from us and never return!'

And the golden hare swam through the dark water all night long. As dawn broke, she saw land looming upon the horizon. Weary and heartsore, she swam towards it. Finally she crawled exhausted on to the sand and she fell into the deepest of sleeps.

When the golden hare awoke she saw another hare, whose fur was white as ice and who was sitting upon the sand by her side, watching her with the kindest purple eyes.

'What is this place?' asked the golden hare.

'This is Lathrin Island,' the other hare replied. 'All are welcome here, golden hare.'

And, filling the fresh island air, came the voices of hares – bronze and gold and silver; blue-eyed and black-eyed and green-eyed. 'You are welcome, golden hare. You are welcome,' they sang.

So the golden hare stayed and made a home of it.

Some say that she lives there still, and that if you catch a glimpse of that golden hare you'll have good luck through all your waking days.

Dara rested the book on his lap and looked back out at the sea; he tried to imagine a hare, a golden hare, swimming all that way. But how would a hare know the safe way to cross? How would an animal know the way to avoid the invisible currents of the Swathe that dragged even boats out to sea? Or how would a hare know to avoid the Needle Rocks that lurked underwater, unseen, all around the island's shore? Dara felt a sudden flash of rage searing through him.

It was stupid. It was stupid and impossible. He'd always believed in these stories when he was little. He'd believed in the ridiculous Golden Hare and the giant owl who got turned to stone and the old lady who was a secret smuggler. He snapped the book shut. '*The True Legends of Lathrin Island*,' he spat. Even the stupid title didn't make sense. True stuff was true. And legends were made up. That was just a fact. He'd been a fool, a great big baby, to believe in it. Any of it. A stupid hare and a stupid happy ending. It was time he grew up and stopped believing in ridiculous, untrue, impossible things.

Suddenly he hated *The True Legends of Lathrin Island*. He flipped open the stupid, beautiful book again and stared furiously at Charlie's '*Happy 7th Birthday, Dara!*' writing on the title page.

With a little gasp, Dara ripped the title page clean out.

Then he tore out the next page.

And the next and the next and the next, letting each page fall on to his bed one after another after another, until he'd torn out the whole of 'The Secret Smuggler'.

Dara could hear the far-away laughter of children playing on the beach, splashing in the sea, running in the dunes.

Page by page by page Dara ripped the stories from his book – 'The Porpoise Road'. 'The Swan Children'. 'The Banshee Moon'. 'The Owl Rock'. Until only 'The Golden Hare' remained, looking little and lost in the fatness of the empty binding. Dara sat marooned in a sea of paper. In his hands flapped the almost-empty cover of *The True Legends of Lathrin Island*, still glinting with stars.

Dara looked at what he'd done and he didn't cry. He felt cold. And heavy, like he had been transformed into basalt; igneous rock like Lathrin Island; red-hot lava turned hard with time. Lathrin Island. Dara blinked. The plan he'd had since forever played itself for the millionth time in his mind, clear and unchanged. Calm settled upon him. In a way nothing *had* changed. He still knew exactly what he wanted to do.

Ripping 'The Golden Hare' out of the cover in one chunk, Dara shoved it under his pillow, then he got up and reached under the bed for his backpack.

Dara unzipped his bag and packed his water bottle. His binoculars. His phone. His spare puffer. His raincoat. A change of socks. A change of pants. His waterproof torch (he checked it first – circle of light under the bed – it worked). His wallet, with a five-pound note in it. His penknife.

He felt so level-headed and primed and steady he

imagined himself almost like an army commando or like a spy or …

No. Dara shut down the imaginings. He was done with stupid, made-up stuff. He unzipped the pocket where he kept his puffer and his lucky brass hare. The stupid pointless hare peeped dully up at Dara. He shoved the packet of pink pills on top of it and zipped the pocket back up again. There was no such thing as luck. And legends weren't true. He was fed up with waiting and hoping and dreaming.

He opened the door and went to the bathroom; he could hear the TV on downstairs. He brushed his teeth, brought his toothbrush back to his room, packed it. Dara checked his oxygen level. It was good. He dressed, put his warmest red hoody on, slung his backpack over his shoulder, went to the door.

Dara looked around his room at the mess of paper. No – he couldn't leave it like this; when Mum and Dad came in to check on him they'd know immediately something was up.

When Mum and Dad came in to check on him.

Dara thought for a moment. Then he snatched a blank endpaper page from the floor and wrote on it: DO **NOT** DISTURB. He stuck it to his door.

But just to be sure, he gathered up all the other pages

and scrunkled them each into a ball and shoved each ball under his duvet, sculpting the shape of a sleeping Dara.

A different Dara, a Dara he should've been, could've been, would've been …

But wasn't.

Real Dara looked out of the window at the golden evening sky and narrowed his eyes at Lathrin Island. He glanced down at the scrunkled page in his hand – it was the stupid little map from the front of the book; Dara shoved it in his pocket.

Silently he opened his door and crept out on to the landing. He tiptoed down the stairs, past the triangle of light and the TV voices that spilt from the open living-room door. In the kitchen Dara took two bananas from the fruit bowl and the box of matches from the shelf by the cooker. Dara swallowed. Wishing. Hoping. Waiting. He'd had enough.

Dara slid his feet into his embarrassing yellow wellies and slipped out of the back door of Carn Cottage, closing it behind him with the quietest little *click*. He walked away through the dunes; the wind tumbled his hair and the long grass whispered.

He was going to Lathrin Island.

THE GREAT PLAIN

The wind made whisperings in Mothgirl's ears as she trudged onwards, up and up the slope of Carn Hill, pushing her way through the girl-high grass. Foot-worn and weary, her whole body ached. Her spirit ached too as thoughts of Pa and Vulture and Hart panged her, spear-sharp.

Hanging her head, Mothgirl blinked again through the truth of her own rememberings; for the whole of her long journey from home to here, she had seen no trace of Hart at all: no sign of his waymarker, no footprints in the mud; no strand of his hair snagged on a twig; no spat-out fruit pips or left-over nutshells. Nothing. She sighed. The sighing winds breathed around her.

ByMySide's sudden-sharp bark cut through the air. For a small moment, Mothgirl paused; her wolf barked again. But it was not his bark of warning, ByMySide had made his 'Come! Look This!' bark and Mothgirl's heart lifted; with the last of her energy she ran through the grasses until finally she stood, next to her wolf, upon the summit of Carn Hill.

Spreading her arms like eagle-wings, Mothgirl let the wind cool her hot skin. She looked back beyond the grasses, over the long way they had journeyed, all through the night then all through the day: the glint of river marked her path as it twisted and turned, appearing and disappearing, through the great forest. Far off, she could just see the outline of her very own Spirit Stone on her very own hill; it seemed a tiny pebble from here. 'Home,' she murmured and even the word was smaller now too.

Mothgirl turned and looked out beyond Carn Hill to where the river spread, broad and slow and gleaming, across the Great Plain. The wind flapped at her deer-skins and tugged at her hair and Mothgirl sighed – this place was so wide and vast and strange; was Hart here at all? Surely Vulture had not spoken truth. Surely Hart was not truly gone.

The sinking sun lit the dusty flatlands red as embers so even shadows were dim, and suddenly Mothgirl remembered a game she and Hart used to play in the forest, back when she was a small small girl. '*Make light*,' breathed Mothgirl, making the echo of her brother's long-ago voice in her own. '*If you are lost, my sister, make light and I will find you.'* And Mothgirl's mind filled then with the rememberings of how she would run in the darkness, leaving a trail of glowing moonmoss amongst the trees for her brother to find her by.

And he always did find her.

Mothgirl smiled at the remembering of how she would hide in the ferns, and listen to her brother's foot-steps drawing closer as Hart followed her trail of light through the darkness. Her giggle-squeal of joy when he found her. The sleepish comfort as he carried her home to their hut upon his back; she was as small then as Eelgirl was now. So long ago.

Mothgirl's heart ached for her brother – if only she had a pouch full of moonmoss now! If only Hart would see her light and find her and they could return home together to send Vulture running. If only all would be as it was before.

'Where you, Hart?' whispered Mothgirl as she squinted right out to the furthest fringes of the Great Plain where Lathrin Mountain loomed. She shuddered. No. Vulture must have been filling their ears with untruths when he said that he had seen Hart's way-marker out there at Lathrin Mountain. Why would Hart ever think to go to that dark place where restless spirits roamed? Hart was brave but he was not foolish.

And she was not foolish either. She tightened her jaw

and gazed out at the jagged craggy shape of Lathrin Mountain, looming dark and dreadful, right where the river melted and was swallowed completely by the Big Water. The sky beyond was streaked blood-red, bruise-dark and amber – the colours reflected in the far waves like a warning.

'Ha!' said Mothgirl aloud as suddenly she realised. She knelt by her wolf and whispered her new thought in his flicking ear. 'It is a trap, ByMySide. A trap! Vulture wants us to go to Lathrin Mountain to get snatched by spirits. But we will not trip into his trap, my wolf.'

But ByMySide only answered with a 'HHHRRFF' and a toss of his head; he did not care for spirits and warning colours. He cared for meat. Ears high, he eyed the shadowy grasses and bracken on the hilltop for signs of small life.

His nose twitched and Mothgirl saw the gleam in his eyes which showed that, even though his pack was two-legged and hairless, he was wild-wolf still. He licked his lips. A meal was near.

'What creature you smell, ByMySide?' breathed Mothgirl, peering hard into the dim shadows of the rustling grasses. 'Juicy boar? Tender deer?' Her empty belly rumbled.

ByMySide shrank low to the ground, nostrils wide,

eyes aglow and trained on a bramble clump. Mothgirl followed his gaze, spear raised.

The whisper of leaf on leaf. The tiny crackle of small paw on dry ground. And from beneath the clump of brambles snuffled a cautious, listening rabbit. She nibbled grass, fast as fast, and even in the dim of the evening shadows, Mothgirl could see her fear in the nervous way she peered about her, like she always half waited for an attack to spring.

And the wolf sprang.

He was arrow fast, all fur and teeth and claws, but this rabbit was quick and ready! She leaped away from ByMySide and as she bounded into the light Mothgirl saw that she was not a rabbit at all; she was a hare; long-legged, tall-eared and with fur of a colour that Mothgirl had never seen before in all her days in the forest – not nut-brown like other hares, but pale as honey. And the hare was foolish as well as strange for she did not flee back to the safety of her twisted-bramble shelter; no, she leaped down the dusty slope of Carn Hill, with ByMySide bounding behind her.

A fine long hare would make good good eating; Mothgirl tightened her grip on Voleboy's spear and joined the chase. She charged, tumbling over her feet and righting herself again; the hare a bright shadow, her wolf a grey blur, Mothgirl ran fast as fast, and as she reached the flatlands she ran quicker still and she yawped then too! High and wild!

ByMySide howled in answer to his girl and together they ran out on to the vastness of the Great Plain, dry dust rising in red puffs from the thuddings of their fast fast feet.

But the hare was faster.

Mothgirl dug her heels into the earth and skidded to a halt. Panting, she fixed the running hare with her eyes and raised her spear. Aiming near the yellow-thorn bush where the hare would be in the next moment's time, she shaped her throw in the empty air and she was just about to hurl her spear when the honey-pale hare stopped.

Ears tall and alert, the hare turned and faced Mothgirl. And Mothgirl gasped. Her spear arm wobbled. ByMySide stopped running too. For the hare's eyes were blue.

Blue as lightning. Bright as stars.

'Spirit hare!' breathed Mothgirl. Awestruck and fearful, she shaped the make-safe circle sign with her fingers, for protection. She had heard tell of spirit creatures in Pa's firestories but she had never seen one in true flesh. And still the spirit hare stared with watchful star-blue eyes.

Suddenly Mothgirl realised: the spirit hare was not

staring at her; she was staring beyond her. Then Mothgirl's ears heard what the hare had heard first.

Heartbeat deep and deeper. A rumbling beneath her feet and in the air all around. She turned from the spirit hare. And Mothgirl's breath caught in her throat as she saw what made the thunder-dark distant din.

Behind them on the Great Plain rose a huge cloud of sunset-red dust, big as a mountain. Mothgirl squinted at it, and within its billows and swirls she spied the dim shadows of horns and tails and hooves and heads, thrust from the dust and gone again in an instant.

'Aurochs!' she gasped, breathless with awestruck fear.

Aurochs! A whole herd of huge long-horned aurochs were stampeding across the Great Plain! Mothgirl could feel the pounding of their hooves in the ground, like the rumblings of riverfalls after big rain, but louder, louder, louder!

And she cried out in terror and she turned and she ran. For the cloud of thundering aurochs was coming closer, unstoppable and mighty. The herd was charging towards Carn Hill! Towards her!

THE WAYWARD WAY

Dara glanced back at Carn Cottage – its cosy glow so warm and welcoming, calling him in from the dimness and the shadows of the rolling empty dunes.

No. He would not turn back. All his life he'd planned this, and now he'd finally realised that it was up to him and him alone to actually make it happen.

Over there on the other side of the sunset-streaked waters of the strait, Lathrin Island waited patiently for him, bruise-dark and brooding.

Dara turned and made his way towards the harbour. He took the far path through the dunes, the one that ran nearer the field than the strand; Charlie had called this the Wayward Way because it was the sneaky path that Mum and Dad couldn't see from the cottage. Dara didn't take sneaky paths; Dara always told Mum and Dad everything; Dara was always careful. Sensible. Well … until now.

As he trudged through the dunes, Dara played today over and over in his mind. A wolf? What had he been thinking? And what was Dr Da Silva thinking anyway? Cancelling his whole operation just because of one stupid heart flurry! One stupid mistake! He felt the lava-heat of anger bubble in the pit of his belly once more. He'd show them.

Suddenly Dara stopped, blinded by a flash of realisation. He *would* show them. He'd show them he was perfectly well enough for the Big Op.

He'd get to Lathrin Island. All by himself. He'd get home. All by himself. And he'd be totally fine. He'd do it *his* way. And he would prove them all wrong.

He grinned and walked on, imagining how Dr Da Silva would phone them back and say she'd made a mistake and actually Dara could have the Big Op after all and she'd say how sorry she was and everything. 'My apologies, Dara,' he murmured half under his breath, in his most purrish Dr Da Silva voice. Then he giggled. Everything was going to be fine.

Suddenly his giggle froze.

What was that noise?

It stopped almost as soon as it started. A low moan, like someone in pain.

Dara peered out over the darkening dunes, thinking of the stupid wolf howl that he definitely did *not* hear earlier. 'Hello?' he called.

Silence listened.

'Is there – is somebody there?'

But nobody answered. Just the whisperings of dune grass and the distant swoosh of waves breaking on the beach. Dara swallowed. His mouth had gone all dry. He was being ridiculous; it was just … the wind … or a …

The rustle and crack of someone moving through the grass. Footsteps. Coming closer.

Dara staggered away, off the path; his foot sank into a rabbit hole. He lost his balance and he fell back with a thud into the hard sand. He breathed deep; his nostrils filled with a smell, strange but familiar, sweet but rotten too, like fields and zoos.

Coming towards him through the dunes loomed a shadow. Dara scrambled to his feet and faced it.

AUROCHS

Mothgirl had to escape the stampede. Her bare feet pounded the dust as the thick, warm smell of aurochs began to overtake her, bitter like leaf milk, sweet as deer droppings. Mothgirl coughed as she ran towards the spirit hare, thickening dust tickling her nose, filling her mouth, stinging her eyes. The thundering of hooves grew noisier and noisier still, until she could not hear her own fast breath. Mothgirl looked up and saw the sky was vanished in the cloud of red dust; her feet were gone from beneath her, and ByMySide was …

ByMySide!

Mothgirl's pounding heart jolted. She skidded to a halt. Where was he? Where was her wolf? Panic rising, she rubbed at her streaming, scratching eyes with her fists, sightless in the deafening dust.

'BYMYSIDE!' she screamed. 'BYMYSIDE!' But her

desperate voice was lost amidst the thunder of hooves and snortings and bellowings.

The earth shook beneath her feet: the aurochs were close; they were many! Flame-fast terror rose in her: she was so small; so small, so alone, so foolish!

Mothgirl ran again, unseeing, choking with dust-breath, but in her panic she did not know if she ran towards the rampage or away. She turned, she saw a flash, a blink of star-blue, spirit-bright eyes, she changed direction, ran towards them. She could feel her voice screaming but no sound came out, only the crashing roar of aurochs.

Something heavy and fast struck her hip; ByMySide! He hurtled into her with such force that her legs crumpled beneath her and her whole body thudded to the ground. She rolled through dust and sharp tearing branches. And ByMySide rolled with her; she smelt his smell and felt his fur on her skin.

In a whoosh of stink-thick air the herd were there. Mothgirl curled her body tight around ByMySide, together in a ball, while all around them hooves stampeded in the choking red dust.

Mothgirl pressed her face tight to his fur, covering her head with her hands. The stampeding storm of aurochs' hooves was everywhere, she felt their wiry hairs scratch her arms and the damp warmth of their bellowing breath. But she did not look up. At any moment a hard black hoof could crash down upon them and crumble their bones like nutshells. She shook with sobs as the trembled ground rumbled beneath her.

She heard the deep-fear growl ByMySide made in his belly and she clutched her deertooth necklet; she tried to sing spirit song to make safe but Mothgirl was choking, breathless in the dust-thick air.

And through the din came Pa's voice whispering from a firestory told in the depths of her rememberings. *One day our waking days will end … one day spirit sleep will come and take us all …*

'No, Pa!' she sobbed. She did not want her waking days to end. That was not the way!

She lay curled tight as a bud with her trembling wolf and tears streamed hot from the darkness of Mothgirl's closed eyes. Her sobs lost against the mighty racket of the aurochs, who huffed and snorted to one another as they rampaged, shaking the earth and the air all around.

BEAST

Breathless with fear, Dara squinted at the looming shape in the dusk. The shadow approached. Massive. A beast.

He felt his chest tighten. He tried to stay calm. He did the breathing exercises Dr Da Silva had taught him.

In; two ... three ... four ...

Out; six ... seven ... eight ...

Then the shadow made the noise again, the long low moan.

And suddenly Dara started to giggle, his fear lifting like birds from a branch. The shadow was ... *mooing*!

It was a cow! Only a cow.

He knew that the farmer often let the herd graze on the dunes down by the East Strand; one of them must've wandered right up here. Dara grinned in relief as he watched the shadow cow bend her big head to nibble at something delicious in the dune grass, then amble onward, slow and placid.

Dara put his hand on his chest; his heart was *not* slow and placid. He felt a pinch of shame – imagine getting so afraid of a big old cow! He sat down on the grass and had a puff on his puffer. He felt better for all of five seconds, but then the tightness clasped his chest again. Dara eyed the cosy glow from Carn Cottage – he couldn't exactly turn back now after a sunset stroll through the sand dunes and a close encounter with a cow.

He turned the packet of new pills over in his hands. 'The Pink Pills of Power,' he murmured, rolling his eyes. Mum had said to take one at bedtime and one in the morning. Maybe if he took one now it'd be enough to stop his heart from going bananas as he rowed across Lathrin Strait? Dara whooshed his pill down with a gulp of water, then put everything back into his backpack.

Everything except his little lucky brass hare, which had rolled and fallen, unseen, on to the sand beneath a yellow-bloomed gorse bush … and lay there still. Poised and ready. Alert and listening. Forgotten in the coming dark.

YELLOW-THORN

Mothgirl lay curled in the dust, one hand buried tight in ByMySide's fur, the other clinging to Voleboy's spear.

Ears ringing, head spinning, Mothgirl chanted spirit song while visions of all that she loved swirled through her mind like a night story – Hart and the moonmoss, Pa by the fireside, Eelgirl in the tree, Owlboy and his jump-stones. 'No!' and 'No!' and 'NO!' she whispered hoarsely, spitting dust from her mouth. She would NOT let spirit sleep take her; she needed to find Hart; she needed to fight Vulture; she needed to return to her family. Mothgirl tightened her body and gritted her teeth.

She felt ByMySide wriggling; he made a noise like he was arrow-struck. Mothgirl cried out too and she gripped him harder. A wild stinging wind whooshed fast around her, and suddenly the air was thick with smells, new smells, like water weed and salt fish. And through the ringing of her ears Mothgirl heard new sounds also. Not the thundering of hooves and the snorting of aurochs but small quieter sounds – the *crikk-crrrik* call of a night creature and the soft rustle of wind in reed-grass.

She felt ByMySide's muscles soften in her loosening arms. Mothgirl rubbed the sand from her eyes and, opening them, she lifted her chin and stared up into the pale blue sky of early night which glowed through a web of thin branches above them.

Mothgirl squeezed herself from beneath the scratchy twigs and crouched, coughing, on the sandy ground. Mothgirl looked back at the place she had crawled from, where ByMySide still hid; a small hollow at the base of a yellow-thorn bush – here they had lain, safe from the stampede, sheltered amongst the prickle-tangle of branches. 'I give thanks,' she whispered hoarsely to the yellow-thorn bush.

And lowering her face to peek into the hollow, she reached out her hand to her trembling wolf. 'Oh, ByMySide,' she breathed. 'I give thanks to YOU, my wolf.' For he had saved her; his clever nose had found her in the whirling dust and sent her tumbling into the shelter of that yellow-thorn hollow! She reached in her arm and rubbed his fur and sang to him softly until his fearful shiverings eased.

Her wolf crawled out then too. His ears flat and

frightened, his tail tip twitching, his amber eyes darting, firefly fast. He pressed himself to her, leaning so strong and heavy that Mothgirl near toppled once more.

ByMySide opened his jaw and dropped something on to her lap. He softly made his dig-find noise. *Look! Look this!* He fixed his girl with wide amber eyes.

'What you find, ByMySide?' whispered Mothgirl as she lifted the dig-find from her lap, still warm and wet, walnut-small and pebble-hard. She held it high to catch the last of the light.

And she gasped, in horror and in awe.

For it was a small small hare, cut from a stone so strange and cold and gleaming it made Mothgirl shiver just to look on it. Impossibly perfect, a honey-pale 'Spirit hare?' breathed Mothgirl, her voice catching, for she was sudden afraid.

She turned the gleam-stone hare over and over in her hand and she shivered deeper, thinking of those bright blue, other-world eyes. How? How could it be? Mothgirl could knap a fine flint spearhead, she could draw the line of a fast fast deer on the cave wall, but no man, no woman, could ever make stone take the shape of a creature, so small and so perfect. Her mouth was dry with fear. No – it was impossible. It was too strange. Spirit-strange.

So with her spear-strong arm Mothgirl flung that

small small impossible spirit hare from her, up and over the grey grasses, furthest far away.

Mothgirl reached for her wolf, but ByMySide sprang from her in a cloud of pale dust, chasing his dig-find far into the night.

Mothgirl ran blindly after, calling out his name, her voice drowned by that harsh *crikk-crrrik* of a bird she had never heard before.

BANSHEE MOON

Crrrriikk ... crrrikkk! came the raw lonesome cry of a corncrake. Dara stood still a moment; on tiptoes he squinted in the dusky light to where the bird was calling, over in the long grass beyond the dunes.

The Wayward Way dipped down past the Old Boatshed. He and Charlie used to sit in here and read on rainy holiday days. Dara ran his hand along the flaking paintwork. He kind of felt sorry for the Old Boatshed; now that the New Boatshed had been built on the other side of the harbour, hardly anyone kept their boat here any more; it was all just abandoned and uncared for. Dara glanced out at the seaweed-strewn slipway and the poor old sea-battered jetty. Dara rounded the side of the boatshed; out-of-date posters for craft fairs and sandcastle competitions were pinned to the closed door and billowing in the breeze. Dara lifted the padlock and, biting his lip, he tried last year's code: 4242 – the lock clicked open. 'Yes!' he hissed under his breath. He drew back the bolt and pushed open the squeaky door.

Inside, the air was salty and stale, like it hadn't been breathed for a long, long time. In the dim light, Dara could make out the shape of a wonky-looking old boat perched on a stand to get fixed; all around the shadowy walls was a jumble of boxes and heaps and piles and dan-gly bits of who-knows-what.

Dara swallowed, trying not to imagine eyes watching him from the darkness or voices in the wind that whiz-zled through the cracks. He stepped into the Old Boatshed, fumbling in his backpack for his torch.

From the dark above his head came a rustle-kerfuffle and a whoosh of movement, and Dara screamed and ducked and stared after the shape of a pale white barn owl who flew off into the darkening sky. Dara steadied himself. *Only an owl. Only an owl.* 'Sorry, Owl,' he whispered.

His circle of light danced through the shadows until it landed on the orangey warmth of a heap of life jackets, stacked in a crate by the cobweb-thick window. He went to them and rummaged through the cool, clammy pile until he found a Dara-sized life jacket; he put it on and was turning to go when he heard a bark somewhere beyond the boatshed.

Dara spun around and peered through the salt-fogged glass – there, at the top of the tallest dune, silhouetted by the rising moon, stood a huge shadowy dog. Dara squinted across the smooth vastness of the silvery strand; where was its owner?

The beach was empty.

Dara looked back and blinked at only the moon. The dog was gone.

Or perhaps it was never there at all. A tingle tiptoed between his shoulder blades. The door squeaked in the wind.

He hurried out of the Old Boatshed, closing the door behind him with a bang that scattered a whole flock of dune birds.

He found the path once more and climbed slowly up the final sand dune to where the Wayward Way met the viewpoint. Dara stood, catching his breath, and looked out to where a huge full moon was rising above the dark water. 'The Banshee Moon,' he whispered under his breath. 'The Banshee Moon' was one of the spookiest Lathrin legends – when he was little he used to have to sleep with the lights on and his fingers in his ears after Charlie read it to him, because in the story it was hearing the banshee's wails and sobs that had the power to trap you underground forever. Dara shuddered, in spite of himself.

'Just a stupid story,' he muttered crossly, and he turned away from the stupid Banshee Moon to face the bright hustle-bustle of the harbour.

A fishing boat was coming in; Dara watched as the crew tossed big ropes to the shore men, calling out to each other over the raucous cries of the circling gulls. There was a queue at the fish and chip shop and he could hear laughter and music spilling out from the open doors of the pub. Some older kids were kicking a ball on the little patch of grass by the car park; just noisy shadows, and swathes of fairy lights twinkled around the ice cream kiosk where two up-late little ones ran round and round a lobster pot in small gigglish circles.

Dara eyed the empty boats bobbing in the harbour. Then he looked at all the people milling around, and laughing and eating and playing. He'd never thought it would be so ... busy. Suddenly in the harshness of the bright lights and busy-ness and the music his head started to spin and his plan started to crumble.

What had he been thinking? *Just borrow a boat from the harbour.* What a stupid plan!

He'd never even rowed a boat for more than a few strokes! He'd sat with Dad in little dinghy over at Horseshoe Bay last summer, watching Mum and Charlie jump off the high rocks; Dad had explained how to row and even let him have a tiny turn. But ...

Dara looked out at the moon-dappled path between the buoys that led through the waves all the way to Lathrin Island. Other people would be able to row all the way to the island. '*Other* people,' he whispered bitterly, looking down at the footballing teenagers and the round-and-round toddlers. But not him.

When he was little he'd believed in everything: all Charlie's stories; all the *true legends*; all the impossible dreams.

Dara laughed a tight, bitter laugh. He remembered saying that he'd sail around the world one day, single-handed. That he'd climb to the top of Mount Kilimanjaro. That he'd make a raft and go down the Amazon River.

'One day,' Mum had said. *One day.*

Then Dara had started shrinking his hopes. Maybe he'd climb up to the top of Ben Nevis. Or he'd sail across the English Channel. He'd take his raft down the River Bann.

One day. One day. After the Big Op, Dara.

He remembered telling Tam in school that *one day* he'd row right across to Lathrin Island and see the Golden Hare, and Steffan Baxter had overheard and said he bet a million pounds that Dara never would because the Golden Hare didn't even exist and everyone knew Dara Merriam had a jelly heart. And Steffan Baxter got in big trouble and had to apologise. But he didn't mean that apology; Dara remembered seeing him cross his fingers behind his back.

Suddenly Dara felt all alone in the world. He looked down at himself in his stupid yellow wellies and his stinky old life jacket, with his ridiculous backpack, packed with pointless things. What had he been thinking? Perhaps this wasn't the way things were supposed to be after all. Perhaps *he* was wrong and Mum and Dad and Dr Da Silva were right. Perhaps even horrible Steffan Baxter was right. And facts were facts. There was no Golden Hare. And Dara Merriam couldn't row across to Lathrin Island.

Beneath the ominous brightness of the big low moon, Dara sighed. And far, far below him, the dark waves sighed too.

CHANGED

Mothgirl followed ByMySide's paw prints through the moonlit sandhills. Sighing winds breathed around her. *Whisper and hiss. Whisper and hiss.* She climbed higher, looking low, and suddenly her eyes narrowed.

Here at the top of the sandhill another track crossed ByMySide's trail. A strange track. Almost like man prints. But without toes. She knelt on the cool sand and ran her fingers over the prints. She shook her head. 'Foot deerskins?' she murmured. Mothgirl had heard tell of foot deerskins worn by clans from the far-ice-lands, but she had not believed that could be truth. Yet here were the markings, clear as the paw prints of her very own wolf.

But the clans from the far-ice-lands were danger clans – vicious and cruel. They had strong, strange spirit powers and hearts cold as snow. Mothgirl shuddered. Had a man from the far-ice-lands stepped *here* where Carn Hill met the Great Plain? And if indeed he had, then was he here still?

She stood slowly, tightening her spear grip, and, for the first time since she and ByMySide had crawled from beneath the yellow-thorn bush, Mothgirl looked out across the Great Plain. She staggered backwards, gasping at what she saw.

Where once there was dusty red earth and tangle-grass and yellow-thorn, where once there was aurochs herd, and rabbit burrow and a wide slow river ... now – now – the Great Plain had vanished.

She shook her head in astonishment, her legs weak as grass. For as far as she could see stretched the moon-shimmered vastness of the Big Water. That whispering wind: it was not wind at all; it was the Big Water filling the air with its own noisy breath!

And Lathrin Mountain? She blinked at its looming shadow crags, out there on the edge of everything. Lathrin Mountain was no longer itself at all. It was ... an island. An impossible island.

Mothgirl felt her throat close in terror. How could this be? How could this be?

She turned slowly, weak as ash, and in the pale grey moonlight Mothgirl saw that all her world was changed.

Small lights twinkled everywhere, some moving, some still, like the very stars had tumbled from the sky.

As Mothgirl gazed back at the way she had journeyed, she felt bitter sickness rise in her throat. Because ... oh ... what had become of her forest? Where were all the trees? Where were the forest creatures? Where were the deer and the boar and the bears? Where were the soaring eagles and the leaping lynx? Where was her home?

A bird circled white in the dark sky above her; *ACCCCKKK-ACCCCKKKK-ACCCCKKK!* it called, and Mothgirl shuddered at the remembering of Vulture's cruel laughter.

A slow-spreading tingle crept though Mothgirl's bones; cold as fear; hot as anger. She wiped her eyes with her arm, then she started to run. Dizzy and stumbling, she ran through the sandhills, shaping the make-safe circle with her fingers at all that was bright and noisy and new. *How? How could everything simply be ... gone?* She needed to understand.

But most of all she needed to hide.

DOOR

ACCCCKKK-ACCCCKKKK-ACCCCKKK! taunted a gull wheeling in the blue-dark sky.

'Shut up!' mumbled Dara, rubbing roughly at his furious, disappointed tears with the back of his hand. Through the blur he saw stupid Lathrin Island, always there, just out of reach, like it mocked him. Dara turned his face away, bitter and ashamed.

He trudged back along the Wayward Way, his life-jacket straps flipping and wriggling around him like sail ropes in the wind. He stomped down the path and round the bend to the Old Boatshed and ...

Dara froze.

The door of the boatshed was open. It swung in the wind on squeaky hinges. He *knew* he had closed it earlier. He remembered the bang of it, loud enough to frighten those birds. He was one hundred per cent certain – that door had definitely, double definitely, been closed.

An icy chill sneaked through him. So why was it open now?

He blinked. No light came from the boatshed.

He listened. No noise either. Just the surge of the waves and the whoosh of the wind.

Squinting his eyes to see better, Dara left the path and crept through the spiky grasses towards the Old Boatshed. He tiptoed closer. Alongside the building now, he peeked through the filthy salt-smeared window. Inside was darkest dark.

Dara shivered. *Silly. It was silly to be afraid*. He gave himself a little shake. All he had to do was pop the life jacket back, then he could head home and crawl under the covers and give up on stupid everything.

Slowly and silently he crept round to the front of the boatshed, where the door still swung like a loose tooth. Dry mouthed, he peered in through the dark gap.

All was still and dim and so silent he could hear the sound of his own breath. *Silly*. There was nothing in there. He had nothing to be afraid of. He glanced up towards the darkness of the owl roost; not wanting to disturb her again, he didn't flick on his torch this time. His eyes would adjust.

Cautiously, slowly, Dara stepped inside.

Dara blinked in the darkness. It smelt like weather-worn wood and salt and night, familiar and secretive.

'Hello?' he whispered. 'Is there anybody in here?'

No answer. Just the *squeaky-squeak* of the door in the breeze. He took another step. He held his breath, listening.

His blood froze.

From deep in the darkness of the boatshed Dara could hear the soft sound of someone breathing.

'Who are you?' he squeaked. 'Who's there?'

BOY

Mothgirl did not understand. She stayed low and still, watching the boy who stood in the moonlight at the entrance to the wooden hut, just a small spear throw ahead of her.

The boy's hair was short as lynx fur! And, although he seemed no taller than she was, his shadow chest was puffed up, impossibly broad and strong, and from it dangled thin snakes that danced and wriggled all around him. She glanced at his feet, remembering the tracks in the sand – *foot deerskins! He was wearing foot deerskins!*

The strange boy spoke his strange words again, louder now. '*OOO-WAAA-WOOO? OOO-S-AIR?*'

And though the words had no meaning to her, Mothgirl made their shapes with silent lips. And suddenly Mothgirl understood what had happened; it all fell into place like fragments of a shattered rock pieced together once more.

This strange boy was an invader from the far-ice-lands! It was *he* who had made the Great Plain vanish and it was he who had turned Lathrin Mountain into an island! She trembled in the dark, shaping the make-safe circle with one hand and tight-grasping her spear with the other. The invader had spirit powers but, she gave silent thanks, he did not have night sight it seemed, for he had not seen her ... yet.

Fear pounded in her heart as the invader took another step towards her in the dark. And another. Her mouth went dry. She needed to escape. But how?

The invader stepped forward once more, but his deer-skinned foot caught on something and he fell on to his knees with a shout and a crash of falling sticks. Mothgirl saw her chance.

All of a rush, she leaped to her feet and sped, lightning-quick, out of the dimness of the hut and into the bright moonlight. Dazzled and dizzy with fear she ran forward; away! Away! Her feet slapping the hard, damp ground, she looked back over her shoulder, and then droplets splashed and she felt the cold on her ankles and Mothgirl gasped.

No! She had run straight into the Big Water. She

paused, breathless and terrified as the wind tossed her hair and stung her cheeks.

Before her were the white-froth, night-blue waves.

But behind her loomed the invader from the far-ice-lands. He waved his arms at her and shouted his dreadful words that moved waters and shrank mountains and made stars come tumbling down from the skies.

Mothgirl screamed in terror and ran forward into the dark coldness of the wild waves.

GIRL

Dara's eyes widened. He waved frantically at the girl. 'Stop!' he called. 'STOP!'

But the girl in the sea didn't listen. She ran-stumble-splashed down the slipway into the dark water.

'STOP! PLEASE!' he yelled, waving at her frantically. 'YOU CAN'T SWIM HERE! IT'S DANGEROUS!'

Either the girl didn't hear or didn't care; she just glanced over her shoulder and hurried faster, deeper, slipping and stumbling forward until only her top half was above the waves, the pale cloak she wore across her shoulders bright in the dark water. What was she thinking?

Everyone knew the currents were fierce and unpredictable if you went too deep. Dad said that even in a boat it was almost impossible if you weren't following the route between the buoys. Dara's skin prickled with fear; what was he supposed to do?

He stared helplessly up the strand – but the long beach was smooth and silver and empty. He couldn't get all the way to the harbour in time. Fumbling desperately in his backpack, Dara pulled out his phone. No signal at all! He flung it back into his bag and ran out on to the little jetty. Half hidden beneath it, a tired little boat bobbed in the dark.

The girl was kind of swimming now, but a weird splashy doggy-paddle, like she couldn't even swim properly.

'Come back!' called Dara, his voice a weak squawk in the wind.

The girl went deeper and deeper, beyond the jetty, away from the buoys.

Dara stared in powerless horror as a big dark wave pulled itself up to enormous hugeness just in front of the girl. It was about to break! Dara couldn't bear to watch … but he couldn't look away either.

The wave lifted the girl high upon it, up, up, until she vanished clean over the top, then the wave broke, crashing with such force that Dara gasped.

Where was she?

As the white foam and spray slowly settled, Dara saw her small dark head come bobbing to the surface.

'Hey!' he shouted. 'Swim back this way! Please! You have to get out of the water!'

If she didn't, then another big wave like that one could push her under, or snap her clean in two. Next time she might not be that lucky.

Then Dara saw another dark shape amongst the froth and the waves – less far out; swimming ashore it seemed. Was it a seal?

But as the shape reached the slipway, Dara realised that it wasn't a seal; it was a dog. Dara swallowed. It was the huge dog he'd seen on the dunes through the boat-shed window.

The dog ran out of the sea up the slipway; he didn't look quite so enormous now that he'd been in the water, his wet fur clumped into little hedgehog spikes. But still Dara started backing away slowly as the dog ran at him, claws skittering noisily on the slippy wood of the jetty.

Dara heard the *clonk* of the dog dropping something at his feet. Then the dog looked at him, expectant eyes amber like fire. Dara bent and picked up the something. He stared at it in astonishment – it was his hare, his little brass hare, the hare that he'd thought was safely tucked in his backpack.

'What the ...' He shook his head at the huge dog in astonishment. 'How did you get my h—'

But before he could finish, the dog had fastened his

111

teeth on to the hem of Dara's hoody and was tugging at him.

'Get off!' said Dara, shoving the hare into his pocket and trying to pull his hoody away. The dog's teeth were bigger than any other dog's teeth he'd ever seen – they looked like proper fangs. Dara staggered back, afraid, but the dog held on, tugging again and again at his top.

Finally the dog released him and, opening his fangy jaws wide, he made a noise which froze Dara's bones to their very marrow: it was the wild low cry he'd heard on the strand that afternoon; it was … a howl. A howl so hollow and so wild that Dara's helpless shudder told him the truth, clear as air.

This was not a dog; this was a wolf.

And this was *not* his imagination. The wolf was as real as he was; Dara could smell his wet fur and his hot breath. What was an actual wolf doing here?

The wolf made a noise deep in his throat and looked at Dara for a long blink of time, his golden eyes so heart-sore and fiery that Dara could read them like a story: the wolf was asking him to help the girl. Because if he didn't, then she was going to drown.

DARK WATERS

Mothgirl's head sank beneath the waters.
Roar and tumble.
Writhe and thrash and shriek and howl.

Wolf howl?
ByMySide?
Mothgirl's face broke the surface

GASP

Stinging breath
Not enough

Big water, angry, darker than a bear, tall
like a mountain

How?

GASP

How could this be only
water?

The wave, grew, loomed, peaked …

… crashed

… smashed

… spun her around

… pressed her down

… down

… down

… dark

… down

… deep

… down

… silent …

Make light, said Hart's lost voice

I cannot, she answered in the dark

Mothgirl breathed out.

Her last breath,

a bubble

moonbright,

floated up …

through the dark water …

up …

up …

and was gone …

PEAGREEN

This was more than *not a good idea*. This was a truly terrible idea. Dara knew it already as he untied the stinking, weed-slimed rope from its mooring ring. He didn't know how to launch a boat or row a boat or steer a boat or anything, but terrible idea or not, it was his *only* idea. And he had to act fast or the girl would get swallowed up by the sea and that would be the most terrible thing of all.

He felt the tug on the rope as the waves lifted the boat and dropped her again. He squinted at the faded writing on the hull of the battered old boat. *'Peagreen!'* he said aloud. Like in that poem 'The Owl and the Pussy-Cat' that they'd learned off by heart in school.

But Dara didn't have time to think about it; *Peagreen* seemed seaworthy ... ish.

Dara left the rope looped loosely around the mooring

ring while he climbed down the ladder and stepped into the boat. The bow lifted up with his weight and cold fear surged through him. Dara swallowed. Gingerly he shifted to sit on the little board bench in the middle of the boat and it all balanced up again.

He could feel the wolf watching him from the top of the ladder as he fixed the oars in their rowlocks. Dara looked up and met his golden gleaming eyes. 'Wish me luck,' he said to the wolf, and he pulled on the rope, tugging it free from the mooring. The rope slapped down on to the floor of the boat and almost immediately *Peagreen* started drifting away from the safety of the jetty, towards the wild waters beyond where the girl was –

Hang on – where *was* the girl?

Dara craned his neck and peered desperately into the night, scanning the rising-falling dark waves for her. But, nothing. Was he already too late?

With a sudden wood-splintering crash the boat lurched, the stern dipping dangerously low in the water. Dara screamed as he was flung forward on to the floor. Had he hit something? He turned around, dazed, and came eye to eye with the wolf.

'What – ? How – ?' stammered Dara, clambering back into his seat. 'Did you just jump off the jetty?'

The wolf simply blinked and made his whining noise,

which Dara now understood. His noise meant: *Come on! Hurry up! Find my girl!*

Dara twisted his head and fixed his gaze upon the spot where he'd last seen the girl; he grabbed the oars and he pulled. All those times he'd watched longingly from the shore as Dad and Charlie went out on fishing trips in the little dinghy – he could do it. Leaning forward, he lifted the oars clean out of the water and, leaning back, he pulled again.

The boat cut through the water; it was working – he was doing it! The sea splattered his cheeks and soaked his arms; the wind whirled his hair. The wolf was at the bow of the boat now, nose forward, like a furry, fangy figurehead. And Dara, he was actually rowing into Lathrin Strait – just like he'd always wanted to do. He plunged in the oars and heaved.

The sea was getting rougher as they moved further from the jetty; the little boat lifted up, up, up, and dipped suddenly down. Dara felt the lurch in his belly. They climbed another wave; from the summit Dara stared wildly around, searching for the girl, but he could see no trace of her – only water; only darkness. Dread prickled sickly beneath his skin. The wolf was making his desperate whimpering noise, scanning the water too ... but ... nothing ...

Hang on – what was that? Something was floating over there in the water …

Peagreen plunged from the top of the wave with such force that the bow dipped into the swirling water. The wolf leaped back, his claws scrabbling on the floor; Dara clasped the side of the boat and dug his heels in to stop himself from falling. The boat righted itself, but water sloshed and rolled in a little mini-sea of its own over Dara's feet.

Dara peered frantically into the water, looking for the dim shape he'd too-briefly seen bobbing on the moonlit surface.

'Hey!' he screeched into the crash of waves and the roar of wind. 'Where are you? Hey!'

But no answer came.

Then Dara saw the shape again, floating on the surface. The wolf barked in short, harsh *yarp*s as Dara heaved on the oars. Bringing them closer. Closer. Until they were right alongside.

But it was not the girl at all.

It was her little fur cape, the one she'd worn around her shoulders. It floated on the dark water, empty and forlorn.

LEAP

'Nononono!' said Dara, leaning out of the boat to try and catch the bedraggled cape. But a wave snatched it from him, plunging it under. As Dara withdrew his hand he realised how much he was shaking.

Wiping sea spray from his cheeks and eyes, Dara noticed how the wolf's front legs were trembling too as he leaned forward, peering desperately into the churning water.

From nowhere, a huge dark wave crashed into the other side of the boat; water gushed in and Dara gripped the bench as *Peagreen* rocked violently from side to side. Dara could see another monster of a wave building; he had to turn the boat around to face it before the wave broke. He paddled ferociously and the boat started to twist. Then from behind him the wolf suddenly began to bark.

'It's all right,' gasped Dara. 'Don't worry. I've seen that wave. I'm turning! I'm turning!'

But the wolf kept barking, frenzied and urgent. Dara felt a tug on his hoody; he looked down; the wolf was pulling at him.

'Get off me!' He yanked his hoody away. Then his eyes met the wolf's eyes and suddenly he understood. 'What? Where? Where is sh—'

The second enormous wave struck *Peagreen*, sending her spinning. Dara shouted and sprawled forward on to the deck, still clasping the oars. He looked up.

The wolf's forepaws were balanced on the rim of the boat as if he was about to …

'Don't!' Dara yelled.

But the wolf just glanced back at him and made a sharp, decisive bark. Then the wolf leaped overboard, an arced streak of grey in the dark sky.

Dara heard the *splosh* of his landing; he scrambled to the edge of the boat and, gripping the rim, peered into the churning sea, just in time to watch the white tip of the wolf's tail disappearing beneath the pale foam of the waves.

He felt sick. *No! No! No! No! Stupid wolf! Stupid girl!* A choked sob came hiccuping out. Dara suddenly noticed how tight his chest was. *Stupid heart – so stupidly stupidly stupid!*

Still crouching low, he tore off his backpack, yanked open the pocket, grabbed his puffer and gulped at it. Lightness for a second. Breath. Easy breath.

Then the smack of another wave spun the boat around. Dara flung his backpack back on his shoulders and grasped the oars tightly. He peered into the water, hopeful and hopeless at the same time – but no sign, no sign at all. The girl had been gone too long, surely? And now the wolf was gone too. Dara was all alone.

He pulled on the oars, not sure any more which way was the shore and which way was out to sea, but he had to do something; he had to go somewhere. He gazed desperately up at the swinging stars through tear-hazed eyes. Then Dara felt *Peagreen* tilt and he heard the huge sighing suck of the sea. He turned just in time to see a towering wall of a wave grow taller, and still taller again. Dara blinked in terrified astonishment as high, high above him the enormous wave trembled on the brink.

Dara screamed. The wave broke with a roar.

BENEATH

Beneath the Big Water
   in the dim and the still
      Mothgirl felt spirit sleep
        pulling her downwards
           gentle and soft and dark until …

Make light!
Make light and I will find you!

Hart!
She was so close to finding him.
Hart!
She could not give up now.
Hart!
She had to keep hunting.

Mothgirl's eyes flickered open.

A pale glow through the dark water above her.

Moonmoss?

Could it be?

Mothgirl kicked weakly

with the last of her strength

and she rose

just a little

towards the glow

> but the dark waters

>> only darkened

>>> and turned and curled

>>>> tighter around her

>>>>> dragging her deeper

>>>>> Hart?

>>>>> Mothgirl had to …

>>>>> Hart?

>>>>> … keep seeking …

>>>>> Hart?

>>>>> … but she was tired …

>>>>> … so tired …

A tightness.

A tugging.

Someone was pulling her by the deerskin.

Pulling her up …

up …

up …

… to the surface where the wind whirled wildly and where there was moonlight and starlight and noise. Her chest screamed with pain. She gasped and choked and coughed all at once. And in all the dizziness of it Mothgirl saw the swirl of wet grey fur and the bright amber of his eyes.

'ByMySide!' she gasped.

And from deep in her wolf's belly came the proudest, happiest dig-find sound; the sound that meant *My girl! I have found you.*

Mothgirl clung, coughing, to ByMySide. He gripped her deerskin tight-as-tight in his jaws and pulled her through the Big Water.

BOAT

Mothgirl saw the wooden boat and her tired heart leaped.

Hart? Was it Hart? In his canoe?

She let go of her wolf and reached up with her water-weak arms until she gripped the side of the boat; she hung there a moment while her limp body shook with the force of her coughs as water came pouring out of her mouth and she gasped, struggling to stay afloat.

Mothgirl felt hands on her wrists and she looked up into the face of the boy. The strange boy. The invader from the far-ice-lands. No! She tried to push herself away.

But the boy held her tightly and she was too weak to fight him and he heaved and she scrambled with her legs, and something pushed her from behind and then she slid on her belly over the side of the boat to land with a flop on the floor, helpless as a salmon caught on a bone hook. Except a salmon flipped and flapped when it got caught. Mothgirl just lay there, face down, exhausted, coughing, still spitting up water.

Mothgirl could hear the boy speaking, but she could not understand his words.

She felt the warmth of his touch on her arm; she rolled on to her side and looked up at him. He did not have cruel eyes. For a moment she forgot to be afraid. The boy took a strange deerskin from a bag and wrapped it around her; it crunched like fallen leaves. And Mothgirl realised that the invader in his boat had helped ByMySide to save her from spirit sleep.

She slowly sat and hugged her knees. She was shaking. She pulled the boy's deerskin tighter around her, rubbing her arms. The boy was talking to her, gentle-voiced. Mothgirl shook her head. No. His far-ice-lands words were like birdsong or bearvoice. She could not hear their meaning truly.

Then the boy touched his chest; he said one word. Over and over and over again. Mothgirl screwed up her eyes as she listened hard.

Then she pointed to him and opened her salt-dry lips and spoke his name.

'DA-ra-MURR-um,' she said, her voice still rough with coughing.

And as she spoke his name, Mothgirl felt a small something pop deep in her ears, like when you climb so high on a mountain that your ears need to change inside themselves.

'You?' said the boy whose name was DA-ra-MURR-um. 'What's your name?'

And like a fog had cleared, Mothgirl understood his words. She put her shivering hand over her fast-beating heart and spoke her very own name back to him.

Seeing the boy's brow furrow, she said her name again.

NAMES

'Moth … ga?' said Dara, uncertainly. But as he said it he felt a little pop in the back of his ears, like when you're on a plane. 'Mothga?' he tried again.

And the girl crouching bedraggled on the floor of the boat smiled a very small smile. 'Mothga!' she said hoarsely, touching her chest. 'DA-ra-MURR-um!' she continued, pointing at him.

'DA-ra-MURR-um!' said Dara, touching his chest and smiling back. Saying his name her way made him feel less *himself*; stronger somehow, braver, like a warrior.

Mothga turned her head then and looked about the boat, as if searching for something. 'Daramurrum,' said Mothga. Her voice was weak. 'Daramurrum, where my wolf?'

Dara looked over the edge of the boat into the dark water. The wolf!

He scanned the moon-dappled choppy sea but the wolf was nowhere to be seen. Dara felt sick. He searched off the other side of the boat and dread crept through him with a coldness that chilled his bones. No! It wasn't possible. Dogs were brilliant swimmers; some dogs even had webbed feet – he'd definitely read that somewhere; surely wolves were the same?

Dara squinted back towards the jetty because maybe, just maybe, the wolf had swum ashore.

But Dara could see the Old Boatshed clearly in the moonlight. A flock of seabirds stood on the slipway, carpeting its black surface white as if snow had fallen. They would never have settled if the wolf was there.

Peagreen rocked suddenly; Mothga was trying to stand up and look over the side. She was pale and shivering, her eyes hollow as she scanned the moonlit sea.

'Where my wolf?' she said again. Her voice sounded so little and lost that Dara didn't quite know what to say. He bit his lip.

'I think he's gone ...' he whispered.

'Gone? Where gone?'

'Ummmmm ...' Dara's eyes met Mothga's eyes, so dark and so sad. 'Uummm ... gone to ...' He shifted awkwardly on the boat bench. Then he caught sight of the dark shape of Lathrin Island, out across the strait. 'I think he's gone to the island ... maybe ...' He pointed uncertainly across the dark sea. As he spoke he saw in his mind the ridiculous impossibility of the Golden Hare swimming across the strait. Of a wolf swimming across. Of anything crossing that churning belt of water without a boat. And he knew he was lying.

'My wolf?' she murmured blearily, gazing out into the night to the darkest dark of Lathrin Island.

He looked at the girl properly then. She was real, he wasn't imagining, he wasn't dreaming, of that he was certain. But nothing about her made sense: her wet, furry clothes; the way she spoke; her name even – *Mothga* – what kind of a name was that? Maybe she had hippy-dippy parents or something.

'ByMySide!' called Mothga, her voice half drowned out by the wind and the waves. 'Where you, ByMySide? Where you?'

'ByMySide ...' murmured Dara. 'Is that your wolf's name?'

She nodded. Dara saw her eyes swim with tears. 'ByMySide!' she called again, her voice cracking.

BYMYSIDE?

'BYMYSIDE!' Mothgirl screamed his name into the night, so loud it made her throat burn. 'BYMYSIDE!'

Where was her wolf? Her own dear wolf.

As Mothgirl searched, her tears began to fall and her calling voice faded to a whisper. The Big Water was so dark and so vast. What if ByMySide had tired and weakened and …

'No!'

Mothgirl rubbed her eyes roughly. No! ByMySide was full-brave and spirit-strong. He was her wolf; he would not let the Big Water pull him down to the depths.

She peered across the black waves at the island, shadowy and looming. Mothgirl shivered, remembering Pa's firestories – *she* knew never to go to Lathrin Mountain, but ByMySide did not fear restless spirits. Wolves and spirits could drink from the same spring and no harm would come of it. Could this boy, Daramurrum, be right?

The boat rose and fell gently in the dark waters. Mothgirl pulled herself tall, Daramurrum's deerskin flapping noisily about her in the wind. She was alone – no Pa, no Hart, no ByMySide. Even Voleboy's spear and Mole's rabbit-skin cape had been lost in the waves. All she had was her small trembling self. Narrowing her eyes, she watched the strange boy from the far-ice-lands; he watched her back with furrowed brow. He was not of her clan. He was not to be full-trusted.

Mothgirl took a big salt-air breath and fixed her heart steady. ByMySide was on that impossible island so, spirits or no spirits, she would go there too. She would find her wolf and bring him back from Lathrin Mountain, then together they would find Hart and return home. Mothgirl nodded firmly – yes – ByMySide had saved her from spirit sleep three times over. Now it was up to her to save him.

'We go Lathrin Island!' she said to the boy.

Daramurrum looked at her, eyes wide as the moon. 'What? We what?'

Mothgirl pointed across impatiently. 'We go find ByMySide! Give me paddle.' She held her hand out for the wooden paddle Daramurrum was holding.

A sudden wave slammed the side of the boat, jolting

them both off balance. Daramurrum clasped the paddle tight to his chest. 'Ummm … no. We need to turn around and get back to shore, Mothga,' he said. 'You're still wet and you nearly drowned and we should take you to hospital or something.'

Mothgirl stared at him blankly.

The boy spoke again, more slowly. 'We should go back.'

Mothgirl made a little snort and stared at the boy fire-eyed. 'You say my wolf on island, Daramurrum! I not go back.' She sprang to her feet and crouched low. The boat rocked from side to side.

'Stop it! What are you doing?' shouted Daramurrum. 'We'll fall in!'

'Give. Paddle!' said Mothgirl.

'No!'

She lunged at him. The boat leaned and a big whoosh of wave water sloshed in over their feet. They both yelled.

'Mothga!' The boy was breathless now. 'You have to stop. You have to give up. We have to go back. It's not safe – I only said your wolf was out there on the island because I didn't want you to be sad. Nobody can swim across Lathrin Strait – it's too dangerous. Listen to me, Mothga – I'm sorry, but I lied. ByMySide isn't on the island. It's just not possible. Your wolf is … he's …'

'NO!' yelled Mothgirl at the foolish far-ice-lands boy with his foolish words. She hurled herself at him.

Jerking away, the boy thudded off his small seat and the boat dipped wildly and Daramurrum screamed. Mothgirl grabbed the wide end of the paddle and pulled; he tugged back and the nose of the boat rose up and caught on a wave and they spun around and a huge splash of water slapped her full-face, full-throat, making her cough come again, but she did not let go. Nor did the boy. Mothgirl and Daramurrum sat panting in the belly of the boat, each gripping one end of a paddle and staring, fierce-eyed, at one another.

'We. Go. Lathrin. Island,' she said again, her voice low and dangerous.

'That's. Not. A good. Idea,' said Daramurrum slowly, and then, to Mothgirl's surprise, he began to laugh.

'Why you laugh?' she hissed.

THE SWATHE

Dara laughed and laughed, but his laugh was as cold and hollow as an empty egg.

'Why you laugh?' said Mothga again, eyes narrowed.

'I'm laughing because I just realised how stupidly ridiculous this is,' wheezed Dara, shaking his head. 'All my whole life I've planned to row out to Lathrin Island. On my own. And here I am, actually in a boat on Lathrin Strait.' All his bitter laughter melted away now and he felt the hotness of tears waiting behind his eyes. 'Here I am, and it's not how it was when I imagined it. It's not the way I planned at all. It's not all brave and bold. It's stupid – and – impossible – and –' he tried to catch his breath – 'and it's dangerous – and –'

A big wave slammed into the side of *Peagreen* with a crack. They were both flung off balance and Dara felt Mothga finally let go of her end of the oar.

Dara scrambled back on to the boat bench and peered fearfully out into the blue darkness. 'Oh,' he breathed. 'Oh, it's not possible!' Cold realisation swept through him; while they'd been arguing they'd also been drifting. The lights of the town were just pinpricks now and the jetty had vanished into the dusk. They were almost in the middle of the strait. Another wave rocked the boat. 'We have to get back to shore!'

This time Mothga didn't argue.

Dara searched the darkness desperately for the glowing buoys, the markers that showed the safe way back. Then he finally spotted one and his belly lurched; the buoy was pale and small as a bubble; so far across the waves.

'We need to row to the buoys, Mothga!' he panted, his mouth dry. 'Help me!'

But Mothga didn't answer. He glanced back at her; she was curled in a ball in the stern, with his red raincoat wrapped around her shoulders like she'd just given up entirely. 'Mothga?' he called crossly. 'Come on!'

But she just ignored him, her face hidden. A thought struck him. Maybe she was actually crying. Maybe she'd realised her poor wolf was dead. Dara bit his lip. Maybe all her hopes had finally fizzled away too.

'I'm really sorry, Mothga,' he mumbled. But his words seemed thin and useless as paper.

Mothga said nothing. Dara swallowed. It was all up to him now.

Clasping the edge of the boat, Dara peered into the depths of the sea. Where *Peagreen* was bobbing there were choppy waves, white and frothy in the moonlight; he could see the same if he squinted across nearer the shore of Lathrin Island. But in between was a strangely still, strangely moonless band of oil-black water. Peering in, he could see patterns within it, moving like muscle under skin; ominous silvery swirls that pulled together and apart in opposite directions.

'Oh no, no, NO!' he groaned, suddenly remembering what Dad always said when they stood looking out at Lathrin Strait from the viewpoint: *There's an invisible current in the middle there, looks peaceful as a paddling pool, but all the power is beneath the surface – it'd drag you right out to the Sea of Moyle if you let it.* Dad had had a name for it too, that band of water, a sinister name; oh, what had he called it?

'*The Swathe,*' breathed Dara, and he shuddered.

Breathing fast, he clumsily clonked the oars into the rowlocks. He gripped them tightly and leaned back, pulling hard. But this time *Peagreen* didn't move where he wanted her to go. He tried again; it was like rowing through treacle.

'Mothga!' he called. 'Listen, Mothga. I really need your help here! The tide is turning; if we don't work together we're going to get dragged into the Swathe!'

The girl didn't reply. Why wasn't she answering him? 'Mothga? Are you OK?'

The boat leaned into a wave and Dara saw Mothga's head loll back. Her eyes were closed. Her mouth hung loosely open. A thin trickle of blood ran down her cheek. Dara gasped. 'Mothga!'

A sharp rush of terror and dread leaped through him. He pulled in the oars and clumsily scrambled along the deck. Crouching next to her, he nervously felt for her pulse. Her heart was beating, strong as an engine; relief melted through him at the exact same moment as a great big wave broke against *Peagreen*'s side, sloshing their faces with cold water. Mothga's eyes sprang open.

'Daramurrum!' she said groggily. 'We go Lathrin Island!'

Dara almost laughed at her ridiculous stubbornness, but he didn't have time to laugh or speak or anything before he was flung on to his side in the sudden lurch as *Peagreen* swung round in a semicircle, like she was a toy. Sickness swirled fearfully in Dara's belly as, gripping on to the rim of the spinning boat, he peered nervously over the edge.

The water was black and flat as an off TV. Ominously

138

still. But beneath the surface Dara saw the writhing shapes of secret currents pulling and pushing against one another.

The Swathe.

It was too late to turn back to the harbour now. Much too late. Dara plunged the oars into the swirling water and heaved with all his might. They were going to have to make for Lathrin Island.

BIG WATER

Mothgirl gasped as the Big Water twisted and twirled the boat around and about. Faster than even the river in spring when the snow melted and came pouring down from the high peaks. The boat rocked and swayed as it turned. Mothgirl's eyes widened; she had never seen waters like this: waters so wide and wild and dangerful.

Daramurrum had two paddles, not one, and Mothgirl could tell he was pulling on them with all his strength, his teeth tight, his cheeks red. She shook her head – this foolish boy had it all wrong; she had paddled the river often with Hart and she knew the ways of water: as Hart always said, '*Do not fight the water. The water will win all battles.*' Her heart panged at the memory of her brother, so vivid she could almost hear the edges of his voice in the wind. But the sunshine of slow-river days with Hart felt far far from the darkness here.

Daramurrum heaved hard on the two strong paddles, but *still* the boat turned and spun; the wild waters pulling them hither and thither, like the leaf boats Eelgirl and Owlboy sent hurtling down the rapids. Perhaps the waters were pulling them the same way as they had pulled her wolf – she looked to the island. Soon she would be there with him and she would hold her dear, soft ByMySide tight as tight as tight.

And Mothgirl's heart froze – she could see the shape of Owl Rock, high on the island's summit, but it was fast escaping them. The Big Water was dragging them out beyond the Island to where huge white waves roared, big as mountains, strong as aurochs. Panic fluttered in her chest.

She touched the cut on her head. It was a small wound only; Mothgirl tried to pull her fighting strength up from the depths of herself, but she felt empty as a hollow nutshell without her brother, without her wolf. She breathed a big breath. Still some salt water tickled in the deeps of her. She coughed until her eyes watered.

'Are you OK?' Daramurrum had stopped paddling and was watching her, worry clouds in his eyes.

She nodded, wiping her mouth on her hand. 'Oak-ee!' she declared gravely, echoing his word. And somehow, just speaking it, she felt her spirit strengthen. 'I oak-ee,' she murmured softly.

He began rowing again, going nowhere with all his might. Daramurrum; he was a far-ice-lands boy and he was deep strange; he spoke strange words; he wore strange deerskins; he had washed away the Great Plain and made stars tumble from the sky, but ... she listened in surprise to the rasping fastness of his breath. It reminded her of Pa, when his breath-sickness came. She bit her lip. '*You* oak-ee, Daramurrum?' she whispered.

Before he had time to answer, a huge smash shuddered through Mothgirl's bones; something had struck the belly of the boat, something in the water. Daramurrum shouted and Mothgirl shouted too.

'What is it?' he cried.

Mothgirl clutched the sides and peered over into the dark, writhing water.

'I see no thing,' she answered. *Bad spirits*, was what she was thinking.

The boat was struck again, harder this time. Mothgirl's mouth was dry. 'Fast, Daramurrum!' she cried. 'We need leave this place!'

Dara snorted like a boar. 'I know!' He heaved on the paddles, but the boat did not move any closer to the island.

Then Mothgirl noticed a terrible thing. 'Look!' she said. Daramurrum turned his head and looked where she was pointing. They both stared, speechless, at the thin crack in the boat's side; it oozed water like an arrow wound.

Another splintering smash juddered the boat. This time Mothgirl saw what it was that had struck them. Not bad spirits; a tree. A long-ago-fallen, black-limbed tree that twisted and twirled, trapped as they were by the suck of the whirling waters.

The huge underwater tree struck the boat hard as a boulder and Daramurrum called out as he was flung forward on to the floor. He still held tight to one of the paddles but the other had been wrenched clean out of his hand and was sliding out into the –

Mothgirl dived for it; she was fast, pouncing like a lynx.

But not fast enough.

The paddle slipped into the waves.

She leaned over, trying to grab it, but the Big Water was cruel – that much was clear – the waves snatched it from her fingers while the wind wheezed like old laughter. 'Tttschhck,' she swore, trying … and failing again to reach the paddle. Daramurrum, next to her now, tried too.

They both gasped, watching the paddle as slowly slowly the cruel Big Water lifted it high upon a wave then hurled it down at the mighty black tree trunk. Mothgirl winced at the crunch as the paddle snapped in two.

OAR

'At least we still have one oar,' said Dara, but his voice trembled. He held on to the solitary oar and pulled and pushed and pulled again, but rowing one-sided only made the little boat spin ever faster in the dark swirling water of the Swathe.

'Two sides!' shouted Mothga. 'Two sides go straight!'

Dara knew what she meant; he'd seen people canoeing like that on adventure programmes, paddling on one side, then the other. Dara tried, but *Peagreen* was too wide, much wider than a TV canoe; by the time he'd lifted the oar out of the water and wrestled it over his head to the other side they were drifting backwards again.

'It's no good!' he said, panting. He put his hand on his chest. 'And you're no good either,' he muttered to his heart, biting his lip. He could tell his Pink Pill of Power would wear off soon and he couldn't take another until morning.

Maybe someone would come and rescue them – one of the fishing boats? But the twinkling lights of the harbour were just pinpricks now, further away than ever. The island was dark and distant too. Cold terror gripped him. He couldn't deny it any longer: the currents in the Swathe were dragging them out to sea, and not just any sea either – for beyond Lathrin Island was the Sea of Moyle: the bleakest, most dangerous stretch of water there was – the sea where cursed swan children were banished in one of the *True Legends of Lathrin Island*; the sea where, even in real life, the jagged rocks had been snagging ships for centuries, dragging them under, never to be seen again.

Dara stared at the crack in the side of the boat, where slowly, steadily, water trickled in; already there was a puddle rolling over his wellies. As the water seeped in, his hope seeped out. Dara swallowed. They were powerless. They were two kids with one oar in a holey boat in a deadly sea in the middle of the night. He felt his fast heartbeat quickening again. This was the absolute champion of *not a good idea* ideas. What had he been thinking? How had this happened? His doom-dark eyes met Mothga's. It was impossible. They were done for.

But her eyes flashed with determination. 'We need

145

cross the Big Water,' she said through gritted teeth and, snake-quick, she snatched the oar out of his hands, before he could stop her.

'Oi!' he said.

But she ignored him utterly. Instead she got to her feet, his raincoat billowing like a cape where she'd knotted it over one shoulder. She stood, holding the oar like a weapon, in the very middle of the rocking boat.

'What are you doing?' he yelled. 'Sit down, Mothga!'

The boat wobbled precariously; she staggered forward, nearly tumbling over the edge. They both screamed. Another invisible sea-swirl yanked the boat and tipped her backwards again.

'Mothga! Sit down! You'll fall in! We'll capsize!'

But still she didn't listen. She looked at him, her eyes sparking in the starlight. What on earth was she playing at? Had she gone totally bananas?

Dara looked at her bare feet and wild hair and crazy animal-skin clothes. Suddenly a thought struck him: he'd found this girl hiding in the Old Boatshed in the dark; why was she there? And who was she anyway? Maybe she actually *was* totally bananas!

'Sit down! Please!' he shouted desperately and, clutching the little wooden bench with one hand, Dara snatched with his other at the oar, but Mothga dodged easily out of his reach.

The boat lurched again. Dara yelled the worst word he knew. This crazy girl was going to kill them both!

But then, giving him a sharp look, Mothga plunged the oar into the black water and she started to row.

Two-sided. Standing up. Just like that!

Dara's mouth gaped open. She was fast, fast like ... like a professional. He almost felt like laughing. She was like an Olympian or something as she whipped the oar from one side of the boat to the other, like she'd been doing it all her life.

He could feel *Peagreen* starting to pull against the current, resisting the force that was dragging them out to sea. 'You're doing it!' he shouted, grinning incredulously. 'Wow, Mothga! Amazing!' He took off a welly and used it like a bucket to bail out the water.

And Mothga rowed, and rowed, and rowed. And suddenly they weren't drifting away from Lathrin Island any more. They were heading across the Swathe towards it. 'Keep going! We're going to make it!'

But Mothga didn't answer; she was breathing hard, he could hear her puffing and panting even above the wind and the sea. Even if she was superhuman, she couldn't keep going like that forever. They needed to break the

147

hold of the Swathe ... and fast. The problem was Dara couldn't tell where the currents of the Swathe began or where they ended; the underwater world was subtle, unjudgeable, invisible to all but the fish.

A big dark shape leaped from the water, dead ahead, ten metres off; it flipped in the air and disappeared beneath the waves with a pearly splash. Dara and Mothga gasped in unison – it was as big as they were!

Another, further off, no, *two* this time, leaping together like shadow acrobats in the moonlight.

'Porpoises!' said Dara, awestruck. A pod of porpoises!

Dad and Charlie had seen them too one time when they were fishing off Lathrin, and Dara'd got really upset because he'd always desperately wanted to see porpoises; even though he'd only been little then, he still remembered it clearly. Charlie had looked up porpoises in a book afterwards and read aloud to him, showed him pictures and everything, so that he could imagine he'd actually been there too.

Only a few metres away, a porpoise rose to the surface, not jumping this time, only her shiny fin breaking through the star-sprinkled water, smooth and graceful. Dara gasped at how close she was.

Then suddenly Dara remembered: 'The Porpoise Road'! The porpoises in the story liked to play right on the fringes of the underwater currents ... right on the border between the deadly waters and the steadier ones, balanced between worlds.

'Mothga!' yelled Dara.

She looked at him, rowing slower now, her eyes weary but fierce. Then she stared to where he was pointing, to where dark shapes rose and arced and dived, gleaming moonbright in the sea spray. Her eyes widened. 'Big fish!' she breathed.

Dara bailed faster. 'Follow that porpoise!' he yelled.

PORPOISES

Mothgirl dug her paddle deep into the dark waters and turned the boat around to face the big leaping fish. She pulled down and back hard, teeth tight, arms burning like they were aflame.

'Yes!' shouted Daramurrum. 'That's it! Brilliant!' With his yellow foot deerskin he emptied the water that was fast filling the boat, grinning up at her.

But she could feel her strength draining from her with every pull on the paddle, with every swing from one side of the boat to the other. Still the Big Water held them in its grasp. It was like doing battle with a creature who was mountain-big and mountain-strong. Her head began to spin and she felt her eyelids flicker, she staggered forward, dizzy. She could not do this. She could not! She was only Mothgirl; she felt pebble-small, petal-weak against the might of these waters. Her paddling arms softened; the waters were winning; she could not go on.

'No! Mothga!' It was Daramurrum, panic-eyed. 'Keep going! Please! Don't give up!'

But her arms were like slack vines; her chest burned with every breath. She could feel the cruel waters tighten their grip around the boat once more.

'Come on, Mothga!' Daramurrum was afoot now too, standing behind her. 'We're so nearly there! You can do it!' His hands closed over her hands. 'We can do it!'

She shook her head. The Big Water tugged.

'Show me!' shouted Daramurrum. 'My arms are still strong; I've rested. *You* know *how* to do it and I can do all the heaving. Come on, Mothga, show me what to do and we can do it together! Like the porpoises, the *big fish*. They work together too! Just trust me! Try!' She felt him take the weight of the paddle as it pushed against the current.

Out of the edge of her eye, Mothgirl saw two of the big fish leap together out of the water, gleaming blue in the moonlight, perfectly matched like shadows of each other. 'Porr-poss-iss!' she whispered, tasting Daramurrum's strange word on her tongue. *Porr-poss-iss?* What were these impossible creatures? She had never heard tell of *porr-poss-iss* ... but maybe there was more to the world than what she already knew? Maybe there was more to the world than what Pa and Hart knew too?

She felt Daramurrum's hand tighten on her hand and she glanced over her shoulder at the strange lynx-haired boy. 'You can!' he said. His look was flint-sharp but not unkind.

Mothgirl faced the impossible porpoises and with Daramurrum's hands and her hands together they lifted the paddle high.

They drove it down into the dark water, spear-smooth, and Daramurrum heaved, leaning back. They lifted together, and swung and heaved.

Lifted together, and swung, and heaved.

Lifted together, and swung, and heaved.

The boat edged closer to the *porr-poss-iss*, so close Mothgirl could see their small small star-bright eyes watching them back and she could hear their *puff-puff-puff* noises.

They lifted together, and swung, and heaved. Lifted together, and swung, and heaved.

Suddenly the *porr-poss-iss* were all around them. Their dark shapes sweeping beneath the boat through the night waters, then soaring to the surface, and up up into the moonlit air in a shower of shimmering droplets like star-bright sparks. Mothgirl wished Eelgirl and Owlboy could see them – oh, how they would laugh and clap their hands in delight at these fish, bigger than they were, that flew in the sky like wet, wingless birds!

They lifted together, and swung, and heaved. Lifted together, and swung, and heaved. Until Mothgirl felt Daramurrum's grip loosen and she realised that the boat was no longer being twirled and twisted and flung by the Big Water. Instead, small white waves rocked them softly, like they were babies held in arms. Mothgirl and Daramurrum breathed hard and fast.

'We make puff-puff noises,' Mothgirl panted. 'Like por-poss-iss!' And she laughed.

Daramurrum laughed too. All around them waves foamed white like boar spit and the boat rose and fell and rose and fell. Gentle.

'The water not win *all* battles,' said Mothgirl, half to herself. 'Hart not know *all* things!'

'Heart?' asked Daramurrum, his hand on his chest.

'Hart!' she said, making an antler shape above her head. 'Hart my big brother.' She turned to face him. 'First I find my wolf. Then I need find Hart.'

Daramurrum nodded, but his eyes did not understand. 'Where is he? Where is Hart?'

'Hart,' said Mothgirl. 'Hart is ...' She gazed with glazed eyes all around her. 'Hart is lost,' she whispered. She hung her head.

But just then the small boat rounded the headland.

Mothgirl gasped. She pointed wordlessly at a big bright line of light that swept out across the darkness of the Big Water, steady and strong as a sunbeam, then vanishing into the night.

Make light and I will find you.

The line of light swung across the dark water again; Daramurrum pointed at it too. 'Lighthouse.'

'Not *light owls*, Daramurrum,' said Mothgirl. 'That Hart!'

And Mothgirl laughed in fear and joy and disbelief. For this was proof of it. Proof! Vulture had been telling truth when he said he had seen Hart's waymarker. Her brother *was* on Lathrin Island. It was Hart who was lost this time.

And Mothgirl was the one who would find him.

LIGHTHOUSE

'Ow!' said Dara, squirming his arm out of Mothga's too-tight grip.

He followed the line of her pointing finger to where the beam from the East Lighthouse swept out like a searchlight across the dark waves.

Why would Mothga's brother be out there in the lighthouse on Lathrin Island? He couldn't be the lighthouse keeper, there hadn't been any lighthouse keepers at all since all the lighthouses were automated way back when. It didn't make sense.

'Are you *sure* your brother's out there?' asked Dara, giving Mothga a sideways glance. 'Lathrin Island's been uninhabited for about a hundred years.'

'Hart lost,' she said, with certainty. 'Hart lost. I find Hart. I bring Hart home.' She nodded, like a full stop.

Then Mothga lifted the oar and began to paddle towards the island, steady and strong and sure.

Dara sat on the boat bench and took careful little gasps of the wild sea air, but no matter how much he tried to convince himself otherwise, he could tell that the Pink Pill of Power's power was gone now and his chest was starting to feel all locked and tight. He wriggled off his backpack, quickly found his inhaler. Then closed his eyes and took a puff. Better.

He opened his eyes. Mothga was staring at him, curiously, her head on one side.

'What?' he said, embarrassed.

'Breath-sick,' she said with a sharp nod.

'Thanks for the diagnosis, Doctor,' said Dara, rolling his eyes.

Mothga rolled her own eyes back dramatically, then turned to face the island once more. Silently Dara did his breathing exercises, relieved and pleased that his heart seemed to be OK again. For now anyway. He looked at his watch. He just needed to wait five hours and then he could take another pill – so long as he took it easy between now and the morning he'd be fine.

Dara counted in his head and as he counted he gazed curiously at Mothga, at her black-nailed fingers, and at the five thin bracelets on her strong arms, and at the animal skins she was wearing, and at her bare feet, and at her wild hair. 'Mothga,' he asked softly, 'where are you from? Where is … home?'

'Home!' said Mothga, and she turned away from the island and pointed with the oar, back across the silvery black sea. Dara stared where she pointed – all the way back to the mainland, to the moonlit twists of the River Bann, and upstream, right to the furthest hilltop.

'Mandel?' asked Dara in confusion, pointing to the distant orange street-lit glow of the town where he himself was from. 'You don't sound like you're from Mandel, Mothga? Are you sure Mandel is your home?'

Mothga had stopped paddling. She blinked back at Mandel, her eyes clouded and puzzled. 'Is home,' she whispered, her head on one side, uncertain suddenly as she too stared at far-off Mandel. 'Is home and is *not* home. Home is trees. Home is creatures. Home is …' She shook her head like she'd run out of words.

Then she squinted her eyes into the distance and suddenly she grinned. 'Ha!' she said, like she'd won a battle. 'Ha! There my Spirit Stone! You *not* take my Spirit Stone, Daramurrum!'

'What? Your what?'

She jabbed the oar, pointing with it far into the distance to where the Lucozade-orange street-light glow rose above Mandel. 'Ha!' she said again in triumph.

And Dara peered where she pointed. There, clear as a

157

shadow, silhouetted by the neon sky, was the tall standing stone on top of the mound in Mandel Forest. The standing stone that was so ancient people said it had been there since before Mandel was even a town, since …

Dara turned and stared wide-eyed at Mothga. It was impossible. But as soon as he'd thought it, he knew it was true …

'You're from the Stone Age, aren't you?' whispered Dara.

Mothga looked at him like he was totally stupid and totally crazy. '*You* from Stonnidge!' she said with a toss of her head. 'Foolish far-ice-lands boy!' she muttered under her breath.

Dara's mouth went dry. How? What? How was it even possible?

But it was. It actually was possible. It actually was real. He was here in a boat heading to Lathrin Island with a real live actual Stone Age girl. It wasn't how he'd always pictured it, it wasn't how it was *meant to be*, but here he was … Dara grinned to himself in amazement.

A wave slapped noisily into the side of *Peagreen*, splashing salt water into Dara's face. Never mind the standing stone; never mind the Stone Age; never mind who Mothga really was or what she was doing here – one thing for sure, they had to get to the other side of Lathrin Strait and land the boat safely.

'Let's go!' he said, jubilant and ready. But as he turned, Dara saw something coming fast towards them that made him gasp in fear – a wall of sea mist, thick and white as milk.

It swallowed them, swift and silent and strangely cold. Dara shuddered; he screwed up his eyes, peering hard, but all he could see was mist and the dim outline of the wild Stone Age girl.

MIST

Mothgirl took a big breath. Lathrin Island was gone now. Her far-off Spirit Stone was gone now. All there was was the thick white mist that wrapped them round like smoke, like winter breath, like cloud. It was like there was no land at all, no land and no water; no thing. Just he, Daramurrum, and she, Mothgirl, in the leaking green boat.

Daramurrum made a long sigh. But Mothgirl would not let her heart sink with his, not when they were so close to the island, so close to ByMySide, so close to Hart.

Up ahead she saw the hazy swoop of brightness where, deep-buried in mist, the light her brother made still shone on. Her heart soared.

She pulled on the paddle, silently edging through the fog towards the light. Slow and steady. It reminded

Mothgirl of night-hunting in her very own forest, lying await high on a tree branch, not knowing when a creature would come nosing out of the darkness. She stared ahead, eyes alert and darting. If there were strange impossible porpoises here, then what other creatures might lurk in the Big Water?

She shrieked. A yellow-beaked bird swooped down from the whiteness, nearly diving upon them, before he swept skyward once more. Surprised and surprising.

They paddled on through the fog-dulled darkness. She listened; behind the slosh of the water and the whirl of the wind, Daramurrum was making his own music; he made a hum like a bee.

For a small minute she remembered Voleboy, how he played wolfsong on his bone whistle. Wolfsong. She wished she could play wolfsong and call her wolf to safety. 'ByMySide,' she whispered.

And as Mothgirl gazed into the emptiness of the mist, for the first time she let herself think how very far this would be for a wolf to swim. How very strong the Big Water was. Would it even be possible for ByMySide to …

Her throat tightened and Mothgirl quick-pushed the thinkings away. She listened again to Daramurrum's humming. 'What you sing?' she asked him.

'Nothing,' he said. 'Just a silly song my dad used to sing when I was little.'

ee song,' she echoed. Some of his strange words
er to say. Like eating a fresh new fruit.

A sudden high screeching sound and Mothgirl felt the
horrible scrape drawing along the underbelly of the boat;
she winced.

The boat juddered to stillness.

She lifted the paddle out of the water and they looked
at each other, faces pale. They both knew what had happened, but only Daramurrum dared speak it.

'No!' he breathed, dangerously quiet. 'The Needle
Rocks! They're under the water all around the island.
We've sailed right into them.'

The mist thickened, cold on her skin. Mothgirl could
not even see the end of the paddle. A wave lifted the
boat, dragging it further on to the sharp rocks with that
scraping sound that made her teeth twinge and her eyes
squeeze shut.

She looked down. The water was coming in faster
now and their feet were ankle-deep. She used Daramurrum's other foot deerskin to scoop water and slosh it
overboard.

Another wave came, this time a larger one; it lifted
the boat from the Needle Rocks. They cried out together
in joy as the boat was carried free and floated for a breath
until, hearts sinking as quick as they had risen, they felt
the grinding scrape of another Needle Rock beneath

their feet and heard the ear-twisting sound again, like carving a hole in a bone, but worse, much worse.

Wordless with horror, Mothgirl pointed. This time the Needle Rocks had found the very place they were least wanted; the crack in the side of the boat where the dead tree had struck them. Where once there was a thin oozing line, now there was a jagged hole, and through it came a spike of rock that was black and sharp as a spearhead.

A wave shuddered hard into the side of the boat; Mothgirl and Daramurrum screamed. Powerless, they watched the Needle Rock saw a fresh gash in the boat's side, then remove itself as the boat lifted in the next wave and they were flung forward in the tide once more.

'No!' yelled Mothgirl. And through the hole poured cold dark water.

Even though Mothgirl and Daramurrum pressed their hands to it, both of them screaming now, they could not stop the determined water that gushed around their fingers.

WRECK

Dara bailed frantically with his welly. He scooped and tipped, scooped and tipped, but it was no good; the cold water was gushing in so fast. *Peagreen* was definitely tilting now. Dara scooped and tipped and scoo—

A huge wave broke and the boat spun, crashing nose first into another rock. Splintering the wood into pieces. 'Help!' yelled Dara into the endless whiteness of the mist. If Mothga's brother really was at the lighthouse, maybe he would hear them. 'Help!'

The beam of light swung through the fog. They were close now. Really close. 'Help! Hart! Help!' he yelled. Then Dara started to laugh.

'Why you laugh?' yelled Mothga; he could hear the rawness of her fury and her fear.

'Because we're so bloody stupid!' he yelled, hysterical with incredulous terror. 'The lighthouse! The lighthouse is a warning! A big bright sign to say STAY AWAY OR YOU'LL BE A SHIPWRECK, and we've been *deliberately* rowing towards it.'

He could tell Mothga didn't understand, but it really didn't matter. Already the end of the boat was dipping dangerously low in the water.

He felt panic rise in his chest, like sickness. They were sinking.

Dara almost thought he heard a voice. Faint and ghostly. Like the voices of the wraiths and merrows in *The True Legends of Lathrin Island*.

'Help us!' he yelled back. 'Help!'

But no one answered. His legs slid into the cold water and he grasped at the boat bench, but his hands slid and the boat tipped and he screamed and then Dara was in the sea.

The icy zing of it gripped him and squeezed; he gasped, chest tight with the shock, and he waited to sink, dragged down by the waves, but –

He was OK.

He was floating.

Dara looked down. The life jacket, the life jacket he'd got out of the Old Boatshed! He'd forgotten he was wearing it. Dara hugged its squishiness in relief. Hope surged through him like warmth, like sunshine. At least he'd had the sense to wear a life ja—

Mothga!

He peered into the mist and the darkness and the seething white water. Mothga didn't have a life jacket! She couldn't even swim properly.

'Mothga!' he shouted. Where was she?

A big wave surged right over his head, pushing him under. He rose to the surface, gasping. 'Mothga!' he wheezed, breathless, pathetic.

He turned and turned in the dark water, but she was nowhere. His heart was pounding in his ears. He squinted through the mist. 'Mothga! Answer me!'

But all he could hear was the crash and hiss of the breaking waves, and the whistling of the wind and the pounding of his own heart. Then he heard a huge *schlupp* like a giant taking a gulp of water. He turned just in time to glimpse the disappearing nose of *Peagreen* as she slid down beneath the rough-tumbling waves.

WAVES

The cold of the water clasped Mothgirl's chest. Stealing her breath. Stealing her words. She heard Daramurrum call her name but all she could answer was a small small squeak, then a wave crashed into her face and she gasped and she coughed and she slipped beneath the surface.

Her open eyes saw the beam of light cutting through the blurry water.

And Mothgirl knew her brother needed her.

Her legs kicked. She was still holding the paddle. With two hands she gripped that paddle spear-tight, and the paddle floated, and she floated with it.

Up. Up. With a rising rain of white bubbles. Up.

Until she burst through the surface and the cold wind whipped her wet cheeks and she took in a huge thirsty suck of a breath.

Mothgirl kicked and kicked with her legs, holding the floating paddle in front of her, and she swam through the mist. Each wave lifting her and carrying her along, then fizzling flat and dropping her again. She did not know where the waves were taking her. Out to deeper waters or into the shallows.

But she had no choice. She was helpless as a fallen leaf in the river. Exhausted and breathless, still Mothgirl kicked and still she kicked and still she kicked until she felt the suck of a wave pulling her back back back, and she tightened her grasp on the paddle. And she felt the Big Water grab her and lift her high high high on a wave, and for a moment she was above the fog and she screamed.

Because there, straight ahead of her, was a tall spire of rock, sharp as aurochs horn, jutting out of the water. The big tight wave held her a moment and she heard the roar growing and felt the surge coming as the wall of black water bent itself to frothy forcefulness and hurled her forward.

And Mothgirl spun and she rolled and she turned, for a jumble of moments, eyes open, as moon turned over foam over dark, and she felt the paddle smash in her hands on the rocks and she felt herself slide down and down deeper into the quiet blackness.

And in the deep of the dark she thought of her wolf.

Her wolf who had dived down and pulled her up to the surface. Her wolf who had saved her.

Oh, ByMySide! Mothgirl's heart twisted with the truth of it. *Oh, ByMySide!* She had searched the dark water for him, but he was not there. *Oh, ByMySide!* It was not possible for her poor brave wolf to swim all this way. *Oh, ByMySide!* Mothgirl's tears fell, invisible underwater, as she looked truth in its face at last – her own dear wolf was in his waking days no longer. ByMySide was truly gone.

Mothgirl kicked weakly with her legs again. And her toe tips brushed something firm beneath them. Could it be … ? She pushed down with all her might and up up up she rose.

Her face broke the surface. A small gasp and another wave caught her, took her with it, spinning her around and flinging her forward.

Mothgirl landed on her knees. On sand? Sand! Soft sand beneath her! She wanted to laugh and to cry.

A wave crashed behind her, rushing in, tipping her off balance on to her hands. She crawled coughing, through the mist and the waves, until the sand was dry as nut flour beneath her hands and knees. And when she knew she was safe she let her arms and legs soften and collapse beneath her so that she lay on her belly.

Exhausted. Eyes closed. Breathing. Just breathing.

COVE

Dara staggered out of the sea, his knees weak, his breath ragged and raw. His feet sank into the soft sand and he stumbled, then caught himself. He coughed and his cough turned to sickness and he fell on to his hands and knees in the shallows and threw up until he was empty.

Something bumped his foot. Wiping his mouth with his soaking sleeve, he turned around. It was his stupid yellow wellies, both of them, washed up in the tide. He almost laughed as he snatched them up, then dragged himself to his feet and stood wobblish and shivering. The sea mist had drifted way out into the strait. Dara peered into the blue-black waves; he cast his eyes along the wet moonshone sand.

Mothga? Fear filled the empty pit of his belly. Where was she?

'Hhhhuuphhh …' A breath. In the darkness behind him. A hoarse, husky wheeze. 'Hhhhhupphhhhh!'

Dara turned slowly.

He was standing in a little crescent-shaped cove, backed by massive sheer black cliffs and filled with the dark lumpen shapes of seals, grey seals. A whole big colony of grey seals, a hundred of them maybe, and they were all asleep. Big ones and baby ones lay flopped untidily on the sand, their bodies gleaming silverish in the moonlight.

HhhhhuPHHH! puffed the nearest seal, and Dara saw her long whiskers twitch, like she was having a particularly fishy dream. Cold and wet and shivering as he was, Dara couldn't help but grin. Seals!

Then he noticed that one of the seals was not asleep. Just up the beach where the moonshadow of the tall cliffs made everything darker, a big seal lolloped across the sand briefly, then flumphed down into a new spot. Dara wondered for a moment why that seal was awake while all the others slept, then he noticed another shape lying in the shadows over where the seal had been. Dara squinted – what was it?

Avoiding the sleeping seals, Dara staggered up the beach towards the shape, the sand softening beneath his heavy feet. The shape became clearer, more person-like, the nearer he got. Hope began dancing under his skin as the shape became itself properly and Dara could see that it was, yes, it was Mothga! His heart soared. But, as he staggered closer, he realised that she wasn't moving at all. She was just lying there, face down in the sand.

Dara stood, swaying slightly; fresh dread swirled in his belly. He swallowed.

'Mothga?' he said, his voice weak and croaky.

But the girl didn't move. Just a wisp of her dark hair fluttered in the silvery light.

SONG

Mothgirl summoned her strength and rolled herself over on the sand. She opened her eyes and, as she blinked in the moonlight, she saw a grey shape she did not understand.

At first she thought it was a rock, but then it lifted its head and stared at her with big dark eyes. Mothgirl drew back. It was not a rock but a creature, a creature the like of which she had never seen before. Pawless as a fish, but whiskered and wolf-nosed.

Mothgirl tasted the air for the tingle of danger; her spear hand stretched emptily in the sand.

The big grey land-fish did not send her fierce eyes or growlings. He just blinked at her very slowly. *Hhhhh-humppphhhh!* The creature snorted softly like Pa's sleep-breathing.

Hhhhhhhhumphhh! came another soft snort from behind her.

Mothgirl turned with a jerk. Another land-fish lay right next to her. Smaller. Sleeping. Mothgirl crawled to her hands and knees and peered around the moon-pale beach; a whole shoal of land-fish filled the sand, peacefully at rest, *hhumppph*-ing softly.

Then Mothgirl heard the gentle *crunch-crunch-crunch* of footsteps. She spun around, dazed and fearful. But it was not a land-fish; it was Daramurrum. Mothgirl felt a wave of warmth rush through her, like sunlight, like fireglow.

He came slowly to her and crouched by her side in the sand. 'Are you OK?' he said softly.

But he looked so pale and afraid in the blue moonlight that for a small moment he seemed more spirit than boy, and she wondered if he was in waking days or spirit sleep.

She reached out a fast hand and pinched his arm.

'Ow!' he said crossly, rubbing his skin. 'What d'you do that for?'

'Waking days!' said Mothgirl, smiling weakly. 'You in your waking days, Daramurrum!' She held out her arm towards him.

Daramurrum looked at her arm. 'What? What do you want me to do?'

She saw his eyes slowly understand. He pinched her arm too.

Mothgirl felt the sharp zing of living pass fast through her and she let out a little gasp.

Daramurrum smiled too. 'So are you in your waking days then, Mothga?'

She nodded. But her joy to be living was mixed with deep sadness too.

'What? What is it, Mothga?'

'ByMySide,' she whispered, to Daramurrum and to herself.

'I know,' said Daramurrum softly. 'I'm so sorry, Mothga.'

She looked back at him, but he was just a blurrish shape through her tears.

A nightwind blew the sand in spirals. Mothgirl stood on shaky legs and faced the Big Water that had taken her wolf and rocked him to spirit sleep.

'What are you doing?' asked Daramurrum.

But Mothgirl just closed her eyes. It was time. She did not want her dear ByMySide's spirit to roam, restless. And it was up to her to loosen her hold and let him go free into spirit sleep.

She spread her arms full wide, Daramurrum's deerskin flapping noisily about her, and Mothgirl sang softly for her lost wolf, remembering him in all his waking days.

She sang of a girl, four summers old, who heard a small small noise in the dark of a cave, and of how she crawled unafraid into the dark, following the noise, until she came upon a wolf den, cold and abandoned.

She sang with a smile of how the girl found one smallest wolf pup in the den and wrapped him snug in her deerskin, and brought him all the way to her home.

She sang of how when the girl's pa saw the smallest wolf pup he said, 'No! Return him to his empty den! We cannot raise a wolf pup here. Some things are done. And some things are simply not the way.'

And she sang of how the girl, who was small, was also determined, and of how she battled with words and tears and promises until her pa's heart turned.

And Mothgirl smiled through her tears as she sang of how from then on, day upon day, the girl fed her pup with milk flowers and blood beetles until he grew big and wolfish enough to hunt his own prey.

And she sang of how for always the wolf stayed by the girl's side, watching over her with his amber eyes, sniffing the breeze for the coming of harm or of goodness.

And Mothgirl sang of his dig-finds. And of hunts. And of wolfsong. And of yellow-thorn. And of sandhills. And of the cold dark water.

She sang of ByMySide and his waking days. And she cried. And she smiled. And she laughed. And she sobbed. Remembering her wolf.

'I give thanks,' Mothgirl whispered to the wind and

the waves, hoping that her words would find their way to her wolf's long soft grey ears, and that even in spirit sleep he would hear her voice and know that she was with him always.

TRAPPED

Dara bit his lip; he hadn't understood all the words of Mothga's song, but he could hear that she'd sung with her whole heart and every scrap of her soul, like the song was all that mattered. Like the wolf was all that mattered. And he ached with her sadness.

He gazed out into the black water, wiping his cheeks with his hand. 'I give thanks,' he whispered, like an echo.

Mothga gave him a small, sad nod. Then closed her eyes. Dara closed his eyes too and felt the impossible weight of the dark air, thick with unspoken words and thoughts as big as they were, bigger even, bigger than all the world. He thought of the wolf who had brought them here but not made it himself. They had made it because of him. He opened his eyes. And they HAD made it. Against all odds.

The moonlight danced on the waves. The seals snored softly. Far off across the strait the lights of the harbour twinkled. 'Lathrin Island,' he whispered in disbelief.

'Lathrin Island,' whispered Mothga quieter than wind. He looked at her and she looked at him, her eyes were dark as the night sky.

'You cold, Daramurrum!' she said.

Dara suddenly noticed the noisy *chatter-clatter* of his teeth and the trembly-ness of Mothga's hands as she pulled his bedraggled raincoat tight around her own shoulders.

'You're cold too, Mothga!' he said with a small shivery smile. 'We'd better move, we'd better keep going.'

'Where we go?' whispered Mothga, looking beyond the sleeping shapes of the seals.

They stood upon a slim moon of sand; before them roared the vast darkness of the sea; behind them loomed a cliff, sheer and tall and gleaming. Dara peered desperately for some steps or a path or any way out of the bay. But there was nothing. They were trapped.

FIRE

Beside her Mothgirl felt Daramurrum tremble, his breathing too rough, too fast. Sidelong she peeked at his pale pale face.

'Come,' she said, pulling Daramurrum's wet sleeve. 'We need make fire.'

Daramurrum made a small smile through *chatter-clatter* teeth. 'Good plan,' he whispered, and he pointed a shaky finger towards the tall cliff. 'It might be less windy over there.'

So together they stumbled, wobblish and shivering, over the sand and stones, gathering sticks and branches as they went. Warmer just from walking, they reached the dark cliff and Daramurrum opened his back bag with fumbling fingers.

'Oh no!' he said, thin-voiced, as he held up a small wet bundle. 'My matches are soaked!'

Mothgirl looked at him blankly and shrugged. She gathered a small nest of dry wispy weed and laid it on a rock. Then she opened her pouch and took out her fire stones. She felt him watching her like Owlboy and Eelgirl used to do, with curious learning eyes; she knelt and struck and struck and struck the stones together.

A small small spark leaped from flint to tinder and a fine wisp of smoke snaked up into the dark.

'Wow!' said Daramurrum quietly.

Mothgirl grinned and picked up the weed-wisp bundle, blowing on it softly until a small flame flickered.

'Wow! Wow!' said Daramurrum.

'You not know fire, Daramurrum?' She laughed as she laid the burning bundle on the rock once more and fed it with small twigs.

'Not fire like *that*, Mothga!' She could hear the wonder in his voice. This Daramurrum from the far-ice-lands with his foot deerskins and his lynx-short hair and his land all bright with lights, he knew many things, but perhaps he did not know all the things she knew.

She puffed up proud inside and showed him how to gently lay small sticks upon the flames until the fire danced golden and bright. They huddled close to it, warming their blood and their bones and their hearts.

But Mothgirl's belly was not warm; it growled emptily. 'I hungry,' said Mothgirl, eyeing the sleepy grey

181

land-fish and wishing she had not lost Voleboy's spear to the Big Water.

Daramurrum followed her gaze. 'You can't eat seals, Mothga!' he said, eyes wide. He reached into his bag and pulled out two yellowish, moon-shaped somethings. 'Here,' he said, handing one to Mothgirl.

She sniffed it. It smelt between blossom and leaf rot. 'What this?' she said, tapping the moon-shaped something on a rock.

'Banana,' said Daramurrum. 'You eat it.'

Mothgirl nodded. 'Eat it!' she said joyfully, and she took a big bite.

The skin was tough-chewing but the inside was soft and sweet as sun fruit. 'Na-na good!' she said, taking another bite.

Daramurrum laughed a big laugh. He watched her chew, then he too bit boldly through the skin. 'Na-na … good!' he agreed, his eyes wide with surprise.

So they chewed their na-nas until only the too-hard stalks were left; they threw those on the fire, where they hissed and sizzled.

Daramurrum took off his big puffed-up-chest deerskin and hung it to dry upon a rock. Beneath it he wore another deerskin – it glowed red in the firelight, steam rising from its dampness into the night air as it warmed and dried. Mothgirl made a long, wide-mouth yawn. Daramurrum caught it and long-yawned too.

'Snap!' he said, sleepishly.

Mothgirl snapped her teeth. Daramurrum did a snort of laughter.

'You sound like small boar,' said Mothgirl, laughing too.

As their laughter faded, Mothgirl put more dry sticks on the fire and looked at Daramurrum with side-eyes. 'Why you come here?' she asked him quietly.

He looked back at her, a look that was long and deep and gentle and afraid, like the look a deer gives when your spear is raised and she is too close to flee.

Then he stared into the dancing flames. 'I had it all planned, Mothga,' said Daramurrum dreamily. 'I used to lie in bed, plugged into my breathing machine, and think about this island, and work it out; every stage of getting here, I had it all clear, I had it all exactly right in my head – exactly how it was meant to be.' He laughed, but his laugh was not happy, it was sharp and bitter like leaf milk. 'And this wasn't it, Mothga.' His voice was choked and wheezy now. 'I was meant to row out here, by myself. The proper way. The right way. Between the buoys. I was meant to land in the harbour. And run up to Owl Rock. And see the ...'

Mothgirl saw a tear roll down his cheek, amber in the firelight. She touched his arm. Warm and soft as hers. He gave her a smallest-small smile.

'It should've been possible. Everybody said I'd've had my Big Op by the time I turned twelve. I was meant to be better by now, Mothga. I was meant to be like everybody else. I was meant to be … *normal*.'

'What *norm-ill?*' asked Mothgirl gently.

Daramurrum's smallest-small smile grew a little bigger. 'I don't even know, you know? I'm not *norm-ill*, that's for sure!'

Mothgirl's eyes grew wide in horror. 'I *norm-ill?*' she asked, fear-voiced.

'Don't worry,' said Daramurrum, patting her hand. 'You're not *norm-ill* either, Mothga. *Norm-ill* is – like – like everybody thinks everybody should be.'

Mothgirl nodded, thinking of Pa. 'Some things are done and some things are not the way!' she said in a big deep Pa voice.

Daramurrum laughed. 'Exactly!'

'Zak-ly!' laughed Mothgirl back. 'I not norm-ill, Daramurrum! You not norm-ill! Norm-ill is *not the way!*' She clapped his back proudly.

'*Nor-mill* is not the way …' murmured Daramurrum, watching the flames, quiet now with his thinkings.

RAIN VOICE

Dara heard the rain before he felt it. Fat drops falling in small splats upon the sand, in little hissing sizzles on the fire. He held out his hand. 'As soon as we get dry it starts to rain,' he said, looking up at the dark sky. Automatically he went to put on his raincoat, but then he remembered that Mothga was wearing it, tied like a sash around her body, under one arm and over one shoulder.

The fire fizzled and flickered; the rain was getting heavier. 'You should put that on properly, Mothga,' he said, giving the red raincoat a little tug.

She scrunched her brow in confusion. Snatching the raincoat back from him.

'I'm not trying to take it away,' said Dara. 'Look – I'll show you.'

Suspiciously Mothga untied the raincoat sash and

Dara helped her put her arms in the sleeves and do up the front. Finally he pulled up her hood. 'There!' he said.

'There?' said Mothga, looking down at herself, her arms still held awkwardly away from her sides, stiff as a scarecrow.

Dara laughed. 'Move around, Mothga. You'll be dry in there.'

The rain fell even faster now. 'I dry in here!' said Mothga, grinning gleefully from beneath her red hood.

'Well, I'm not!' laughed Dara. 'Come over here, let's try to shelter while the rain passes.' He hopped across the rocks to nearer the cliff edge, where a little overhang protected them from the rain. Dara caught a glimpse of his reflection in the glass-still surface of a sheltered rock pool – he looked different; tousled and dirty and tired and definitely not *norm-ill*, but happy. 'You're on Lathrin Island, Daramurrum,' he whispered to his moon-blue rock-pool reflection with a little smile; maybe Mothga was right; maybe *norm-ill* was *not the way*; maybe there were lots of ways, hidden like currents underwater.

Mothga peered over into the still rock pool too. 'TSSHCCKK!' she said, drawing back quickly with fear in her eyes as she made that little circle shape with her fingers.

'What?' asked Dara. 'What's wrong?'

Mothga peeked again. This time she laughed. 'I not

know me!' she giggled, pointing at her red-hooded reflection. 'I think *who that red red spirit girl?*'

Dara giggled too. 'Who actually are you though, Mothga?'

And Mothga laughed like it was a great joke, but really Dara was kind of serious. What was a girl from the Stone Age doing ... here ... now? What had she come here for? What if her big brother really was lost on this island? Dara thought about the pictures of hairy scary Stone Age men with spears that he'd seen in books at school and he shuddered; they certainly didn't look very friendly.

He jumped. What was that noise? Far off in the water. Was it a voice? He peered out into the night through the lines of rain, listening.

But he heard nothing, just waves and wind and snoring seals. He saw nothing, only the darkness and the moon-glimmered sea and far away the lights of other people.

Far, far, far away.

Dara thought of Mum and Dad then; they'd be sound asleep by now, cosy and warm and safe in bed, back at Carn Cottage. He felt a twist of longing deep in his belly as he stared into the empty night.

No one knew he was here.

He shivered, eyeing the smoking embers of their dying fire over there on the rocks. How was he ever going to get home?

187

BIG CAVE

'Come! Daramurrum! Come quick!' called Mothgirl.
She was perched on a ledge, one-man high on the cliff-
side. 'Look!'

Next to the ledge there was a small opening in the
rock. Daramurrum scrambled up. Mothgirl squeezed
through the gap.

Deep dark.

Mothgirl gave the air a sniff: nothing but the tang of
old fish bones and salt weed; she thought of ByMySide
then, remembering his clever nose that could always be
trusted to smell danger approaching. Mothgirl's heart
panged deep, aching for her lost wolf. She blinked back
her fresh eyeful of tears as she heard the sound of Daramurrum's breathing in the cave behind her.

Mothgirl stared into the dripping darkness, her night
eyes quick to find their way in the moonlight that shone

in beams from rock cracks here and there, turning the walls of the cave black and gleaming, up and up and up. 'Big cave!' she whispered admiringly.

'ECHO!' called Daramurrum behind her into the blackness, and the ringing loops of his voice told her that she was right – *big cave* – tall as her seeking-tree and wide as her whole camp.

She searched the walls of the cave with her fingertips for the carved markings of clans who had been this way before.

Suddenly the cave burst brilliant with light. Mothgirl screamed and covered her face with her hands.

'Don't worry, it's only me,' said Daramurrum's voice. She peeped at him between her fingers. He held a small fat stick and from it shone light, bright as a sunbeam in the cave dark. Blinking, Mothgirl lowered her hands.

'It's a torch,' he said. 'A waterproof torch.'

'Water-poo-tosh!' breathed Mothgirl admiringly.

Daramurrum's laugh echoed and his white-light circle danced on the cave wall. He held the *water-poo-tosh* towards Mothgirl. 'Do you want a go?'

'I go where?' asked Mothgirl, drawing back, fearful that this *water-poo-tosh* might have strange power to carry her away from this cave and bring her to other places.

'No.' Daramurrum laughed again. 'I mean do you

want to try it? Take it?' He held the *water-poo-tosh* towards her again.

Mothgirl bit her lip. 'Hot?' she murmured.

Daramurrum shook his head.

So she held out her hand warily and she took the *water-poo-tosh* from him. Gripping the light maker like a spear, Mothgirl laughed aloud as she swung the beam around the tallest heights of the cave.

'Stop!' said Daramurrum.

Eyes wide and fearful, Mothgirl stilled the *water-poo-tosh*. The circle of light settled high above them.

'Look,' said Daramurrum, pointing. 'There's – there's something up there!'

SMUGGLERS

Mothga held the torch beam steady. High up in the cavern was a little stone ledge jutting out, like a shelf almost. Dara squinted up at it. It didn't look natural, not like the stalactites beside it. It looked human made, deliberate; what was it?

He swallowed; taking the torch back from Mothga, he shone it slowly along the highest cave wall. There wasn't just one ledge; there were loads of ledges and shelves and nooks up there in the dark. He swung the beam down the cave wall; beneath the ledges there was a series of shallow little hollows, like tiny toehold steps almost, worn smooth and unpassable by time or by the sea.

Dara suddenly realised where they were, where they'd washed up; this little cove must be Smugglers' Bay. There was a story called 'The Secret Smuggler' in

The True Legends of Lathrin Island; it was about a tiny, sweet old lady called Gentle Bess who ran the island's bakery, way back hundreds of years ago when people actually lived out here, and who, unknown to everybody, was actually a total bandit. In the story she stashed all her ill-gotten gains – whisky and gunpowder and jewels – in a hidden cavern at Smugglers' Bay.

But Dara had never actually thought Gentle Bess was real or that Smugglers' Bay was a real place. He grinned. Maybe there was even actual loot in this cavern! Dara laughed an echoing laugh and craned his neck, wondering if, hidden at the very back of one of those high little ledges, there was still some of Gentle Bess's stolen jewels, forgotten or abandoned.

Then an idea struck him. Better and brighter than loot. In the story, Gentle Bess never got caught because she hid her loot at Smugglers' Bay in the dead of night, then sneaked back to her cottage through …

'… a secret tunnel,' breathed Dara.

'… seek it tunnel!' echoed Mothga.

Dara shone his torch along the ledges which stretched back and back into the bowels of the cliff, where the cavern narrowed to a cave and then to what looked like …

'YES!' shouted Dara.

The tunnel! Gentle Bess's tunnel!

If the story was true, that tunnel would lead them out of the cave and all the way to her cottage in the ruined village near the harbour. Maybe they weren't trapped here after all.

'Come on!' said Dara, and he beckoned Mothga to follow him into the darkness at the back of the cavern.

WAYMARKERS

'No!' said Mothgirl. 'Stop!'

Mothgirl ran her fingers over the cave wall again, just to be sure. Her heart pounded. 'Give water-poo-tosh, Daramurrum!' she commanded.

Daramurrum's circle of light shifted from the far cave tunnels to where she stood; she heard his soft footfalls approaching. 'What is it, Mothga?' he whispered, handing her the water-poo-tosh.

She shone the light circle upon the cave wall. And she gasped. There was no doubt now.

An antler symbol was carved here in the rock. She traced its familiar branching shape with her finger.

'What is it?' asked Daramurrum, staring at the wall too. 'Is it writing?'

'My brother,' said Mothgirl quietly. 'My brother was here.' She peered closer at Hart's waymarker. It was strangely weather-worn and faded, but she was certain that it was his. She grinned, her own heart soaring. 'Hart is near!'

'Where is he?' whispered Daramurrum, peering around.

'I not know yet …' Mothgirl slowly walked deeper into the cave, shining the light over the gleaming wet walls, looking for more of Hart's symbols so that she could track his path.

Daramurrum followed, looking where she looked.

Sudden as fish-splash she saw it. Another waymarker. There on the cave wall, right at the back where the dark was deepest and the roof was low. 'Look! Look!' She moved swiftly, standing on toe tips to see properly.

Cold horror seized her. The water-poo-tosh slid from her hand and fell with an echoing *clonk* upon the rocky floor. Darkness. Complete and heavy as a cloak.

Daramurrum's sharp shriek. Mothgirl's own shout. Silence. The *drip drip drip* of cave water. The rushing whispers of waves on the shore.

'Mothga?' Daramurrum's whisper, warm in the darkness. 'Mothga? Are you OK?'

'I oak-ee.' Her own voice, small and unsteady.

'What's wrong? Where are you?'

195

'I here.'

She heard his footsteps coming closer, slow and shuffly in the dark. She held her arms out in front of her. Their fingers touched. They both yelped.

'What is it? What did you see?' whispered Daramurrum.

Wordless, Mothgirl took his hand and guided his fingers through the dark towards the symbol carved on the cold cave wall. Shuddering, she traced her finger and Daramurrum's finger together over the lines. It was the same symbol as before – the branching shape of the antler – Hart's waymarker.

But above it was another symbol; a conquering symbol.

She traced their fingers together down the down-slope; up the up-slope. The symbol was in the shape of flying wings.

'What does it mean, Mothga?' breathed Daramurrum.

'Vulture,' she whispered, her voice trembling in the dark. 'This Vulture's waymarker. Vulture is here.'

BATTLES

Dara's eyes widened. 'Who ... or what ... is *Vulture?*'

Then he heard a sound that frightened him more than screams or shouts. The sound of Mothga softly sobbing in the dark.

'What's wrong?' He reached towards her, and finding her hand, he wasn't sure what to do with it, so he patted it awkwardly.

She put her other hand on his other hand and patted his hand in return. Dara felt a little frightened giggle pop out. He heard Mothga make a gigglish snort through her sobs.

'Who's Vulture?' he asked again. And this time Mothga answered. They sat in the velvet-thick darkness and they patted each other's invisible hands and she told him her story.

Dara didn't understand every word, but she told him

a story of clans and of land and of promises and bargains and of her pa who had lost his strength and of her brother who had gone and of the night when a cruel and powerful man came to take her away.

'Vulture!' she said, and she spat when she said his name. Like speaking it had left a revolting taste in her mouth.

'Vulture!' said Dara, and he spat too.

Mothga gave his hand a squeeze and continued. 'So I run and I run and I run with my wolf. We run to find Hart. Hart is big man. Hart is strong man. Hart make safe. We run all the way to here ... to Lathrin Mountain. But ...' Her voice shook. 'But ... I not find Hart ... I not find ByMySide. I all alone.'

'I'm here,' whispered Dara, squeezing her hand back.

'But you not big, Daramurrum. You not strong,' she said.

Dara flinched.

'You have breath-sickness like Pa, Daramurrum. You cannot fight Vulture! You cannot help me.' Her tone was warm and kind, but her words stung Dara, sharp as hornets, cold as ice. He snatched his hands away from her.

'Daramurrum?' she said.

'Don't you *Daramurrum* me!' he snapped crossly. 'You don't even know me, Mothga. You don't even know what I can or can't do! I've spent my whole life with other people making my choices for me – telling me

198

what's possible and what's not. Well, I'm sick of it! Yeah, so, fine, I'm not exactly going to beat Vulture or your big strong brother in an arm-wrestling competition, but it's not all just who can beat who in a fight. There are other ways to win battles, you know? There are cleverer ways, better ways, like in "The Porpoise Road" or "The Secret Smuggler" …'

Mothga said nothing. Dara sighed impatiently in the silent dark. 'Oh, never mind! Right, come on, Mothga! Let's find the torch and go down the tunnel. It's our only way out of h—'

'No, Daramurrum!' Mothga's voice was high and panicky. 'Vulture! Vulture's waymarker! Vulture follow Hart here. That tunnel is Vulture's way …'

Dara's crossness fizzed. She was so sure she was right, but he was sure she was wrong. Her story was just a story. He felt again for the V shape on the wall; it was worn and weathered and ancient. 'Listen, Mothga, if Vulture ever did go down this tunnel, it was probably thousands of years ago. He's hardly still going to be waiting in there, is he? Let's just go.'

'No,' said Mothga stubbornly. 'We *not* go in tunnel. We go other way. You need make new path, Daramurrum!'

'What? What d'you mean, I need to make a path?'

'You not big! You not strong! But you have big, strong powers, Daramurrum, you from the far-ice-lands …'

Dara snorted in frustration. 'I'm not from the *Far Eyes Land* – I'm from Mandel! Listen, Mothga, if you want to go and find your brother some other way, then good luck to you. I have things to do here too, you know, *on my own*. I never planned to come to this island with anyone, least of all a girl from the Stone Age.'

'I *not* from Stonnidge,' muttered Mothga.

Dara ignored her. 'And I don't want to waste my time in a smelly old cave in the dark, looking at scratches on the wall.'

He tried to march off. But the cave was so stupidly dark he had to take tiny little shuffly steps with his arms out in front of him, like a cross between an old man and a zombie. His toe touched the torch and sent it skittering noisily across the rocky floor.

'Daramurrum?' Mothga's voice sounded little and lost. 'Daramurrum? Where you go?'

'I'm going down this tunnel.'

'No, Daramurrum. You NOT go down tunnel. Vulture! Vulture's waymarker! Vulture is near!'

'Pah!' said Dara, on his hands and knees now, feeling for the torch. 'You're just trying to scare me out of it. Nice try, Mothg—'

'Shhhhhhh!'

'You shhhhhhhh!'

'Listen!'

Then Dara heard it too. Clear. Unmistakeable.

The *crunch-crunch-crunch* of footsteps. Walking over pebbles. Coming up the beach. Towards the cave.

Suddenly Dara doubted himself utterly as a horrible thought struck him: if Mothga had somehow come through to his time, and her brother had, then Vulture could too.

Crunch-crunch-crunch.

Dara's hand found the torch. He grabbed it. Pointed it down. Flicked it on. It still worked. He blinked, bedazzled, at Mothga; her frightened eyes met his.

The *crunch-crunch* footsteps came closer. Then they stopped altogether.

Dara flicked off the light and held his breath. He heard another sound, harsh and rattly.

ACK-ACK-ack-ack!

'Why Vulture laugh?' Mothga whispered faintly.

And they reached for each other's hands. Then Dara flicked on the torch, pointed its beam into the blackness, and they ran together through the mouth of the secret tunnel.

TUNNEL

Mothgirl ran fast into the tunnel, her mind spinning in terror. No! No! NO! It was too cruel a truth to bear – she had lost Pa and Hart and ByMySide and now Vulture had found her and was coming for her through the dark. Fear squeezed her breathless. She gripped Daramurrum's hand tight as tight and their feet made *slap-slap-slap* sounds upon the wet stone. Ahead, the circle of light juddered and shook over the sheen of dark rock and the green glow of cave leaf and the pale points of drip stone that hung from above.

Their breath *puff-puff-puffed* together like por-poss-iss. And the tunnel narrowed so they ran one by one now. Mothgirl followed the shadowish shape of Dara-murrum, his back bag shaking up and down as he ran, his breath huffing and catching, rough and ragged.

'Daramurrum?' she panted. 'You oak-ee?'

'I'm OK,' puffed Daramurrum.

But Mothgirl could see how his running feet landed floppishly and how his hands that had been tight fists were now loose and flapping like chestnut leaves in wind.

Belly clenching with fear, she looked over her shoulder. Black as black as black. Like a starless moonless sky. She ran on.

But up ahead of her Daramurrum had stopped. Bending forward, his hands on his knees, he breathed noisily, each breath tearing, ripping so roughly it made Mothgirl wince. She touched his heaving shoulder gently but he shrugged her away. 'I'm – O – K –'

The circle of light was still now, and Mothgirl saw how the tunnel had beams of wood within it, like the poles that she and Pa and Hart cut to build their huts when they made a new camp. This tunnel was not just a cave tunnel, it was people-made, and just ahead it was not just one tunnel any more either, but it forked into two separate ways.

'Which tunnel?' she breathed. 'Which way?'

But the only answer was Daramurrum's ragged breath and another further sound which filled her with ice and horror.

Echoing footsteps from the tunnel far behind them. Not running footsteps. Slow and steady footsteps. The footsteps of a hunter who knew that his prey was held tight in his trap and that there was no need to hurry.

Mothgirl swallowed. Listening. There was another sound behind the slow footsteps.

Step.

Step.

Swoosh.

Step.

Step.

Swoosh.

A remembering of that final night stirred in the dark; her home, her fireside, the giggles of Eelgirl, the sizzle of nutcakes, Pa approaching, ByMySide's growl. The bone-flute music.

And those footsteps in the forest.

Dry mouthed, she heard them as if they were here. As if they were now.

Crunch.

Crunch.

Swoosh.

The *crunch-crunch* of Vulture's feet on the leaves. Followed by the swoosh of his foolish-long bearskin cloak as it trailed behind him. Crunch. Crunch. Swoosh.

Step.

Step.

Swoosh.

'Daramurrum!' she whispered urgently. 'Which way?'

FORK

But Dara didn't know which way. He stared into the one dark tunnel and then into the other and he gasped for breath in the thin damp air and all he could hear was Mum's voice in his head: *not a good idea.*

He wordlessly handed Mothga the torch and fumbled in his backpack pocket for his puffer.

Brief easiness burst gentle in his chest. Like sunlight.

Then he heard what Mothga heard. Slow, dragging footsteps from the tunnel far behind them. She hadn't been making it up! They really were being followed, being chased.

He tried to do his breathing exercises.

… two … three … four …

'Which way?' hissed Mothga.

He tried to think. He tried to think. Tried to think. His head was so foggy. Clumsily he shoved the puffer back in the pocket and his fumbly fingers touched damp paper and suddenly he remembered: the map! The stupid map from his stupid made-up book of stupid made-up stories from stupid Lathrin Island.

That stupid, brilliant, wonderful map.

He pulled it out, gently unfolded the damp paper, turned it the right way up.

'What that?' said Mothga, sounding exasperated. 'Which way, Daramurrum?'

'It's a map; it's *waymarkers*. Shine the light on it, Mothga!'

He landed his finger on Smugglers' Bay, and the Hidden Cavern, then traced the dotted line of the Secret Tunnel until it forked in two and –

'This way!' he hissed, pointing to the right-hand tunnel. And he folded the map into his pocket and he swung the backpack on to his shoulder. 'You go first,' he puffed, and Mothga ran ahead into the tunnel; Dara staggered behind her, steadying himself on the wet walls, which swayed and wobbled into and out of focus.

He swallowed. His heart felt feather-light and bass-drum-loud, all at once. Not a good sign. Not good at all. Dara knew it was one of the warning signals; but maybe if he ignored the feeling, it would just go away.

He shuffled forward, feeling his way along the dark

walls. Mothga's circle of torchlight danced along the tunnel far ahead. He wanted to call out 'Stop! Wait for me!' but he didn't dare, for he could still hear Vulture's footsteps behind him, and if *he* could hear Vulture, then Vulture could hear him.

Dara swayed. He gripped on to the wooden beam that ran along the rocky wall and rested his forehead on the cool stone. He squeezed his eyes tight shut and open again. Little lights were starting to swirl, like fireflies behind his eyes.

'So stupid,' Dara mumbled. He gasped in a big breath. He'd been so stupid. He needed to go home, to get Mum and Dad. What was he doing out here – in a tunnel – on Lathrin Island – in the middle of the night – running – escaping – what was he doing? This was all wrong. This wasn't the plan at all …

His heart raced faster, lighter, louder; faster, lighter, louder.

'Daramurrum …' said a low voice that slid greasily around his whirling head.

Was it Vulture? He couldn't make sense of anything. This was why he wasn't allowed to go on roller coasters or watch scary films or …

Dizzy. Too dizzy.

Dara's spinning blood went ice cold.

The world swayed
and then dipped
and then slammed itself closed
with a cold
dark
thud

STEP-STEP-SWOOSH

Mothgirl looked over her shoulder. Only dark, dripping stillness. No footsteps. No breath. She shone the water-poo-tosh back into the tunnel. Nothing.

Where was Daramurrum?

And – she swallowed – where was Vulture?

Cautious as a rabbit she flicked off the light and crept back along the tunnel, her hand on the cold damp wall. She listened, wide-eared.

Breath. Soft. Fast breath. Daramurrum!

She flicked on the light and there he was, lying on the ground, curled in upon himself like a fern frond, moon-pale, blue-lipped.

She ran to him. Lifted him to sitting. Shook his shoulders. Spoke his name.

But he did not answer. His lynx-haired head flopped soft on his neck like the head of an arrow-struck deer.

She pinched his arm. Hard.

'Owww!' moaned Daramurrum.

Lightness lifted her heart. 'Waking days!' whispered Mothgirl, and she slid her arms under his and pulled him along the tunnel. Her nose so close to his hair it tickled; she sniffed; he smelt of salt and mint leaf and apples. But behind his smell another whiff wafted, faintly, just a wisp in the tunnel air.

And that was enough. It was a familiar stink. The smell of untruth and threat and fear.

The deep red stench of blood paint.

Daramurrum took a big gaspy breath. Mothgirl heaved, staggering backwards on the slippy rock as she dragged him along the tunnel, which sloped up now. She panted as she pulled the boy, who was heavy and floppy as a sack of pebbles.

Aching with tiredness, Mothgirl hauled Daramurrum up the tunnel until ... until the tunnel just ... *ended*.

She lowered him to the ground and felt the walls with both her hands. The walls were all around, apart from the way she had come. The tunnel had led nowhere! They had gone the wrong way!

Tears of tiredness and anger and fear filled her eyes. She fell to her knees next to Daramurrum's slumped body and she buried her face in her hands. It was not possible! Not possible! They had gone the wrong way!

Then her tears froze in her eyes, halfway fallen. Fear gripped her. The smell of blood paint filled the darkness. She held her breath and listened.

Step.

Step.

Swoosh.

The footsteps were close-close. Vulture was nearly upon them. So calm. So unhurried. As if he knew already that their way was blocked.

Mothgirl imagined Vulture smiling his untrue smile, out there in the dark. His teeth filed to points. And she shuddered, sickness swirling in her belly. They had nowhere left to run to. Nowhere to hide.

So Mothgirl crouched, spearless as a small small child, between her friend who lay gasping on the ground and the slow steady footsteps of cruel Vulture. And she waited in the dark, listening for his cackle to come echoing off the walls.

TIPPA-TIPPA-TIP

Dara's eyelids flickered in the dark. He could hear rain falling. He licked his dry lips. Where was he? He reached for his bedside light switch. But his fingers touched cold rock. *What the … ?*

Suddenly he remembered. The tunnel. He was in the tunnel.

But why – why then could he hear rain? He pushed himself up on to his elbows. The *tippa-tippa-tip* of raindrops pattering right above his head. It didn't make sense.

And then suddenly he realised. 'Mothga,' he whispered weakly, his voice so faint he could barely hear himself. 'Mothga!'

'Shhhhhh!' she hissed.

'Mothga! Up! Up there above our heads! It's the way out!'

He heard the crinkle of his borrowed raincoat as she stood. And he heard her grunt with the strain as she pushed up on the trapdoor. And he rolled out of the way of the shower of crumbly mud and pebbles and sand and who-knows-what that came sprinkling down, and suddenly the darkness of the tunnel was shattered with spears of hazy moonlight.

And Dara tasted air. Air so fresh and full of sea spray; wind-whipped and cool and starlit and rain-speckled. He lifted his head to gulp it all in. And he wanted to laugh and he wanted to cry but he was too weak to do anything but breathe and breathe and …

'Get up! Fast fast, Daramurrum!' Mothga's urgent whisper hissed in his ear. And from behind her in the tunnel he heard Vulture's footsteps quicken.

Eyes flickering, he rolled on to his knees and Mothga heaved him by one arm to his feet. He leaned on the wall and felt himself sway as he looked up through the open circle of dark light above him.

'Climb!' hissed Mothga. He heard the sharpness of panic in her voice.

'I can't,' he whispered, with his ghost-pale voice. It was impossibly high. He was too weak. 'I can't.'

'You CAN, Daramurrum!'

And he felt her try to lift him, and he raised his heavy arms and held the edge of the gap, but he didn't have the strength to pull himself up and his fingers lost their grip and he slid back to the ground again.

'I can't!' he wheezed. 'You go, Mothga.'

Without even a pause or a hesitation Mothga scrambled up and vanished through the trapdoor and into the grey-blue night. Her words from earlier played themselves over in Dara's ears: *You not big. You not strong. You cannot fight Vulture. You cannot help me.*

She had abandoned him. Discarded him like rubbish.

Dara lay on his back, letting the rain fall on his face. Powerless, exhausted and empty, he closed his eyes and waited for Vulture's shadow to pass across his face, and for the sharp point of Vulture's triumphant spear to press down upon his chest.

MOTHGA

'Move!' whispered Mothgirl through the moon hole. 'Move! Now!'

She heard the scramble below as Daramurrum rolled himself over, as she heaved the big big stone with both hands until it teetered right on the rim of the hole. With her back she gave it one last big push and it crashed down into the tunnel below.

A cloud of dust rose up through the gap.

'Daramurrum?' she hissed, biting her lip and peering into the moon hole.

'Yes?' Daramurrum coughed and wheezed. Mothgirl's heart soared.

But there was no time for coughing and breathlessness. Vulture's footsteps were only a spear throw away now. 'Get up, Daramurrum!' she hissed. 'Climb up fast, I pull you!'

Daramurrum wobbled to his feet and climbed on to the rock, unsteady as a toddle-child. She stretched down her arms and she grabbed Daramurrum's arms and she pulled and she heaved and she tugged with all her might. And up he came, sliding out of the tunnel and up through the moon hole on his belly. And he rolled away from the gap.

Mothgirl panted as she lifted the wooden circle that had blocked the moon hole and slammed it back down into the gap, piling so many rocks upon it that Vulture would never be able to lift it even if he was the strongest man in all the lands.

'Ha!' she declared. And she pressed her ear to the floor, waiting to hear a cry of fury and disappointment when the hunter arrived only to find that his prey had vanished. But no cry came.

She tossed her head and turned her thoughts to poor Daramurrum, so weak now he had not even been able to use his great far-ice-lands powers to lift himself out of the tunnel and into the light. Mothgirl crept to his side; his eyes were closed again, and even in the pale moonlight she could see the sharp short pull of his breath, the blueness of his lips.

Breath-sickness.

She ought to take him out of this rain. They were in what seemed to Mothgirl a broken hut, made from tumbled stones with no skins upon the roof for shelter, but over by the far wall there was a high jutted ledge and beneath that the ground was dry.

Mothgirl gently pulled Daramurrum to the sheltered place and she took off his deerskin to cover him with. A *hoo-hooot* above made Mothgirl jump; she turned and watched as a white wide-wing owl swooped in the dark sky and found perch upon a hawthorn tree. An idea tumbled into Mothgirl's mind.

Hawthorn leaf! She would make a hawthorn-leaf poultice, just like she did for Pa when his breath was short. She went to the owl tree and gathered hawthorn leaves aplenty. Then she found a flat rock and spread the leaves upon it, before she pounded and pounded at them with a rounded stone. When she'd had enough she scooped up the green leaf paste with an empty shell and approached Daramurrum.

Daramurrum still lay sleeping; he breathed light and fast like the breath of a mouse or a vole. Mothgirl opened her pouch, took out her slicing stone and cut away his top deerskins. She was about to splat the poultice on to Daramurrum's bare chest when she saw the wound he had there, pale and curved like a new moon. She traced it gently with her fingertip. It was an old wound; clean-healed. Mothgirl stared curiously, chewing her lip.

Mothgirl applied the poultice and gently pulled Daramurrum's soft red deerskin closed again.

Daramurrum lay unmoving. She put her ear close by him a moment and listened; if the poultice worked, Daramurrum's rough breath would soon change. She covered him in the crinkly deerskin once more, pulled her own deerskins tight, and she waited, watching the rise and the fall of his moonmarked chest.

'Who you, Daramurrum?' she whispered.

He was not like her. He was not of her clan. He was a far-ice-lands boy who had spirited her whole world to strangeness. Why then had she gone back to him? Why had she saved him from Vulture? And why had *he* saved her from the Big Water? There were many many questions. None of it made sense; clans don't help other clans – it was simply not the way.

Mothgirl sighed and shivered; the rain had stopped but the night air was cool; fast thin clouds swept across the full moon. She wished she could do what she always did when her mind was full of questions: climb high in her seeking tree. But here, in this wind-whipped place, no tall trees grew, so Mothgirl climbed to the top of the stone wall and looked out. No trees grew, but in a hollow between the camp and the craggy island edges there was a wide swathe of stems and grasses, pale in the moonlight.

'Who you … Mothga?' she breathed into the night. Only the grasses whispered in wordless answer.

But she was not *Mothga*, was she?

218

She was *Mothgirl*, daughter of Eagle, sister of Hart. She ran fast in her forest. She was a fine fine hunter. Here in this place she was … she was … strange to herself. Changed as a bramble from bud to fruit.

If Pa was here, what would he say? Would he know her still? Would he call her *My Mothgirl* and rest his big hand upon her head? Mothgirl's eyes filled with tears that made the moon ripple. Would Pa be proud of her that she had crossed the Big Water and reached Lathrin Mountain and saved this breathless boy? Or had she already shamed him too deep?

'Trouble girl,' she muttered; perhaps that was what Pa called her now.

A horrible vision crawled like smoke into her mind. Vulture. How did he know to find her here? Perhaps her own dear pa was so shamed of her he himself had sent Vulture here to capture her and squash her like clay and make her do things the way things had always been done.

If only she could show Pa that there was more … more than … what was that strange far-ice-lands word Daramurrum had spoken? *Nor-mill!* If only she could show Pa that there was more than *nor-mill*. But, Mothgirl sighed, even if she turned around now and returned home, telling Pa of all that she had seen and done and felt, even then she knew he would not listen. 'Firestories!' he would say, as if all this was simply an

219

imagining. No, Mothgirl was just a girl, a twelve-summers-old girl. She needed Hart to make herself be heard.

And Hart needed her – out on the Big Water she had seen the light he made, calling her to find him. But if he was here on this island, why then had his light stopped shining? She bit her lip and thought of the waymarkers on the cave wall. Hart's waymarker eclipsed by Vulture's waymarker. What if Vulture … ?

In sudden horror Mothgirl replayed a remembering in her mind: Vulture's strange fireside promise; his words echoed coldly in her head. *'Vulture will help you find dear lost Hart … Vulture will bring your son to you,'* she whispered. And she remembered the sidelong glances of Vulture's men and their quiet, under-breath *ack-ack-ack* laughter. They had not been laughing at *her*; they had been laughing at her brother and at the fate that awaited him at Vulture's cruel hand.

She sat up on her elbows and eyed the moon hole, covered and piled high with heavy rocks. Vulture was down there in the tunnel, but he would not be trapped there for long. Soon he would find a way out; he was slippery, greasy; he knew tricks and untruths like they were old friends. He helped no one and harmed many, in spite of all his 'kind' words and false promises. Was she already too late to help her brother?

220

'Oh, Hart!' she breathed, and Mothgirl gazed up into the darkness. 'Make light!' she pleaded. 'Make light, Hart, and I will find you!'

At the very edge of her eyes a flash flashed.

Mothgirl leaped to her feet and scrambled up to the top of the tumbled rock walls of the old hut. She watched the darkness, pale-fringed now, way out where the Big Water met the sky.

Sudden. Blink sudden, the light flashed again. The edge of a beam.

She scrunched her eyes, and glimpsed the beam as it swung low across the Big Water; it was coming from somewhere right on the other side of the island.

'Hart!' she squeaked in hopeful joy. Vulture must not find her brother before she did!

And Mothgirl leaped from the wall in a scurry of loose pebbles, landing by Daramurrum, who lay where she had left him; still as still. Mothgirl watched him breathe. Did his breaths come easier now? Gentler? She could not yet tell. But she knew it was best to let him sleep.

So she grabbed a stick and drew a circle in the mud around him. 'Make safe,' she said quietly. 'I will return to you, Daramurrum. I will return with my brother.'

A night bird shrieked, sudden and shrill. Mothgirl ran into the dark.

GLOOP

In his dream Dara heard a whisper, a bird cry, running feet. His eyes shot open.

He sat bolt upright. His red raincoat slid off him on to the muddy floor of – he looked around – the floor of a little tumbledown house, with no roof, that smelt faintly of mushrooms and of sheep and – he sniffed – of something else. Why was he lying, sleeping on the floor of a ruin?

He tried to remember what had happened but his brain felt all muddled and fuzzy. He'd been running … in the dark … in a tunnel … and his heart had …

He put his hand on his chest, just to check his heart was still beating, and – 'Eeewww!' he said aloud.

Sitting up, he peeped beneath his top; his chest was covered in dark green gloop and his hoody had been all ripped open. He cautiously dabbed a finger in the gloop and sniffed it – the goo smelt leafy, earthy, like the potions he used to make with Tam in the garden when they were little. What was going on? Why on earth was he covered in stinky green gunk? Who had … ?

Suddenly everything fell into place in his head: Mothga. Lathrin Island. Smugglers' Bay. Vulture.

'Mothga?' he whispered into the night. She'd pulled him out of that tunnel. It must've been her who'd put this gunk on his chest. He took a big deep breath; the gloop seemed to be helping too, really helping; he could breathe easier than ever before. She'd saved his life. 'Mothga? Where are you?'

But she was nowhere. 'Mothga?' called Dara softly into the darkness as dread crept beneath his skin. Vulture? Had Vulture taken her?

Cautiously he went over to the tunnel entrance. And sighed with relief: the round wooden door was still firmly closed and a huge heap of rocks were piled up on top of it – Vulture certainly wasn't getting out of that tunnel!

Shakily Dara walked out of the ruins of Gentle Bess's cottage. The moon was high and full and everything was painted strangely silver; he wandered through the roof-less remains of what once had been a little village where real people had eaten and worked and chatted and played.

'Mothga?' he whispered. 'Are you here? Are you hiding?'

But all was still. Weirdly windless. The long grey grass on the moon-drenched field only trembled so very slightly. Dara swallowed.

Nothing to be afraid of, he told himself, trying not to imagine stupid, impossible, ridiculous things – banshees and wraiths and cruel laughing men.

He turned away from the village and gazed out to the wide dark ocean. Far away in the east, he could see the very edges of dawn just thinking about breaking; a subtle line of butter yellow where the sea met the sky. Morning would come soon. Maybe as the sun rose all this strangeness would melt clean away and all would be normal again. '*Nor-mill*,' he whispered to himself with a little smile.

Dara blinked into the slow glow of dawn. Was *nor-mill* really what he wanted? A strange realisation tingled in the hairs on his arms and in his wriggly bare toes. Something was ... changing. Perhaps something had already changed.

He had always liked to know what was what. He liked calendars and plans and predictions. He liked knowing what was around the next corner, and the corner after that. But here he was, on Lathrin Island at dawn, and nothing was at all like he'd planned it. Dara hadn't found the Golden Hare, but he *had* found a girl from the Stone Age … or maybe she'd found him. Sometimes it was hard to tell. And sometimes things didn't turn out how you expected them to.

But one thing he did know: Mothga had vanished. And Dara needed to find her again before cruel Vulture found his way out of those tunnels.

Dara returned to Gentle Bess's ruined cottage and crouched down next to the heap of rocks that covered the trapdoor. He listened. No noise came from down there. So where would Vulture have gone? And Mothga? Why would she save Dara's life and then just run off by herself?

He picked up his mud-splashed, gloop-splattered rain-coat from the ground and noticed the circle drawn in the mud; it was right around where he'd been lying conked out on the ground. Mothga must've drawn it. Why?

Maybe it was her … what did she call it? Her *waymarker.* Suddenly Dara realised where Mothga was.

Her brother. His waymarker. *Make light!*

'The lighthouse!' Dara said aloud, looking into the still-dark sky. Out at sea, Mothga had thought that Hart was signalling to her. If he stood on tiptoe he could just make out the lighthouse's swinging glow. He started to run but then thought better of it – some things *could* be predicted pretty accurately, and running was clearly and definitely *not* what his heart wanted him to do.

So Dara slowed his pace and began walking purposefully towards the growing gleam. But something ... something niggled him. Like an itch. Something wasn't right. He glanced over his shoulder at the ruined village, and up at Owl Rock at the headland beyond it. Had he left something behind? He fiddled with his dangling backpack straps; everything was in his bag or in his pockets. Suddenly Dara realised; he pulled the map out of his pocket and, unfolding it, he shone his torch on the paper.

And his belly lurched with fear and horror.

The secret tunnel. The tunnel led from Smugglers' Cave ... and then it forked. The fork on the right led to Gentle Bess's cottage; the fork on the left led straight to the lighthouse.

Dara felt sick. Vulture was down there in that tunnel, and there was only one place he could be headed.

MAKE LIGHT

Mothgirl stood at the foot of the huge, sky-tall hut. She stared up up up to where at the very top of its tallness a ferocious beam of brightest light flashed far out over the black water. This sky-tall hut made her dizzy. Made her belly-sick. It was simply not possible – spirit-touched for sure ... Mothgirl trembled deep-afraid.

But if Hart was there, trapped within its tall stone walls, waiting for her, then Mothgirl would swallow her fear like bitter-leaf tincture and she would go to her brother. Make him safe.

On the outside of the hut was a climbing ladder, like the ones she had made out of sticks and strong-vine for Eelgirl and Owlboy to play on in the forest at home. But this climbing ladder did not sway in the breeze – it was fixed strong to the sky-tall hut and when Mothgirl touched it, it was colder than stone and smooth as ice.

She held on tight and began to climb. If the bright light came from up at the top, then that must be where Hart was trapped. She scrambled, chipmunk-quick, up the ladder, up and up and up until the wind blew stronger, whipping her hair around her head like dancing snakes, like fire flames. And still she climbed.

And as she climbed she thought about her brother. Hart. He had always made her safe. He had cared for her from the day she was born until the day he left their camp. But since dear Mole had fallen to spirit sleep last winter her brother had been ... different ... changed. Sadness had changed him. He had grown quieter and quieter until one day he simply was not there at all.

Mothgirl climbed up and up. Her hands cold now with the touch of the ladder and the chill of the wind. Down below, the island had grown as small as the pebble worlds Owlboy made on the river beach. Mothgirl looked up. And she climbed.

She had tried. All through that long long winter she had tried and tried, day upon day, night upon night, to bring joy to Hart's heart. She had hunted fine boar and sung fine firestories and told jokes that made Pa laugh until his belly wobbled. But Hart ... Hart had stared into the flames. Silent and solemn. Full of his own sadness. Lost.

'Ha!' she said to herself. Her brother would not remain

228

lost. She would find him. She would make him safe. She did not care if Pa said that she was too young and that she was but a girl and that she needed to learn woman ways and make the nutcakes and scrape the deerskins and knap the flints. She would prove Pa wrong; she would be the one to find Hart and bring him home and save them all from cruel Vulture.

Mothgirl glanced down at the dark island in the darker sea. Vulture was out there in all that darkness. He had wanted to find Hart too but … 'Ha!' she said again. She was nearly at the top now, at Hart's bright bright light. *Ha!* Vulture had been too late and too foolish; for here was Hart, making light in the sky-tall hut, and here was she, Mothgirl, going to him to bring him home.

Suddenly she heard a voice.

She looked down down down. A small light danced like a slow firefly on the hillside. *'Water-poo-tosh!'* she whispered. 'Daramurrum!' His breath-sickness was true healed! Perhaps he too would return with them to camp. She imagined Pa's face when he saw Daramurrum's lynx-short hair and his soft red deerskins. 'Not … the … way!' she puffed in her Pa voice.

She waved at Daramurrum and she kept climbing up and up and up until she drew level with the bright bright light. Here the wall was not stone but clear like ice. She shielded her eyes with one hand and pressed her nose to the clear wall's smoothness. Mothgirl peered through, expecting to see her brother's dear face.

But within the high brightness of the hut there was … no one.

Just a light that moved around and around as though it were alive and trapped within itself. A freezing wave rushed through her, colder, deeper, blacker than the Big Water.

Hart was not here.

Mothgirl turned to face the enormous darkness, the beams of light sweeping across the Big Water as if they wiped it clean. And beyond the water was the land she no longer knew and the home she had left behind. Hope fell from her, cold as snow.

Hart was not here.

'Lost,' she whispered into the dark night. And Mothgirl realised that she had lost everything. And that she herself was lost.

Suddenly her head started to spin. Tears filled her eyes. Her hands and her knees began to tremble. She glanced down at the world so far and so dark and so small below and her heart was sudden-afraid. And, fearfully, she shifted her grip on the ladder, and its cold smoothness slipped through her fingers, and Mothgirl felt herself falling.

THE STACKS

Dara screamed. 'Mothgaaaa!'

He gasped in horror, holding his head with both hands.

Then he saw her twist in mid-air, like a cat, and shoot her hand forward; Mothga's fingers fastened tight around the metal and her body jerked to a stop and her scrambling feet found their rung once more.

Dara felt a wave of warm relief surge through him from his toes to his hair roots. He watched as, more carefully now, Mothga found the next rung and the next and the next. He watched Mothga closely as she descended. Something about her had changed; she looked smaller somehow.

Dara tore his eyes from Mothga just for a moment and peered nervously around the barren headland. Where was Vulture? Had he come out from the tunnel already? He swallowed but his throat was dry. The light-house was high on a cliff edge; in the dim early light Dara could just make out the shapes of the Stacks – columns of tall black rock that stood like an army of hunched giants a little way out in the surging waters. There was surely nowhere for Vulture to hide in this barren place? He listened. The wind had dropped and all was still. Just tussocky long grass shivering slightly. Dara shivered too as he turned back to face the lighthouse.

'Keep going, Mothga!' called Dara, squinting up. She was about halfway down now. If the tunnel led to the lighthouse, where would the opening be? If Vulture hadn't got here yet then they needed to be ready for him. He took out the map again, fragile now, and peered at it. But the dotted line that showed the tunnel just kind of stopped.

Dara lowered the map to look for the place where the entrance was marked. Then his heart froze. What was that? He could hear a noise. A ruffling, scuffling noise, soft and deliberately stealthy. The noise stopped. Like it was listening too.

Dara felt sick. He glanced up at Mothga; she was still climbing down the ladder; he really didn't want to startle her. He bit his lip and screwed up his eyes and listened hard. But now all he could hear was the steady boom of his own heart, mixed with the distant thump and shiver of the harsh waves crashing far below at the foot of the cliff.

Then the soft, creeping sound started up again. Ice cold with fear, Dara tiptoed slowly towards the noise, closer and closer, until he stood next to the dark abyss where the narrow headland dropped clean away to the swirling cauldron of the sea below. The noise was coming from somewhere a little way down the cliff face. Surely the tunnel wouldn't open out into nothing, into thin air? There had to be some sort of path. And if Vulture was slowly coming along it, they had to know. Dara edged closer. He mightn't be able to run fast or row far, but he was, thought Dara proudly, pretty good with heights. He lay on his belly on the wiry grass and slowly, slowly shuffled himself forward, until, holding his breath, he peeped over the cliff edge.

And in a whoosh of rushing air and a shrieking screech, something leaped at him. Dara screamed and covered his face with one arm and pushed back with the other. His fingertips brushed something strangely soft; he opened his eyes and saw a huge gull loop out and over the dark waves, then circle back again. Dara glanced down to where the bird had been. A thin stretch of rough path led down to a ledge where a big messy nest was balanced precariously. And then Dara gasped, because just behind the nest was the overgrown opening of a tunnel. Dara quickly shuffled away from the edge just as the bird swooped back to her nest. He took off his backpack and had a puff on his puffer, then he lay panting on his back for a moment before sitting up and checking on Mothga.

She was nearing the foot of the lighthouse ladder now. She was close enough that Dara could see the redness of her eyes and feel the sadness of her heart.

He didn't even need to ask; she hadn't found her brother. Watching her, Dara thought about brothers and sisters; he imagined how he'd feel if Charlie had been lost and desperately needed his help and he'd arrived too late. He felt tears well up in his own eyes then.

He went to Mothga. She jumped the final steps and they stood on hard land, facing each other.

'Hart gone,' said Mothga.

'I know,' said Dara. 'I'm sorry.'

They held each other's gaze then, as the waves crashed in noisy whispers far below. And in that moment they each knew that the other was all they had. Mothga shivered. Dara held out his raincoat; she put it on.

Out on the towering black Stacks, the first seabird woke. Dara and Mothga both turned to look as she cried a harsh and hungry call that woke her mate, who squawked in reply and woke another and another until, before Dara knew it, hundreds upon hundreds of kittiwakes and guillemots and herring gulls were all at once rabblishly chattering and squawking and screeching to each other, so loud he thought his ears would crack. One by one by one the birds woke and waddled or stretched their wings and soared. Like the Stacks had suddenly come alive. But as the huge gulls wheeled above, screaming, Dara heard something else.

A scrambling sound. Cold washed over him. It hadn't been just the gull. They were hearing the unmistakeable sound of someone climbing up from the tunnel entrance towards them.

'Run!' hissed Dara.

LOST AND FOUND

Mothgirl and Daramurrum crouched low behind a yellow-thorn bush. Peeking through the tangled spines and branches, Mothgirl could just see a dim shadow appear at the cliff edge and crawl slowly on hands and knees towards the sky-tall hut.

She squinted in confusion. *Why was Vulture crawling? Was he hurt? Was he sick?*

The dark shape dragged itself into a patch of moonlight and Mothgirl made a choking, breathless cry.

Daramurrum grabbed her arm and for a tiny moment they looked at one another. 'It's ... it's ...' he gasped, eyes wide.

'BYMYSIDE!' shouted Mothgirl, and she leaped to her feet and bounded fast as fast as fast through the pale early light to the soft-grass place where he stood.

Her wolf!

Her own dear true wolf!

'Oh, ByMySide!' she said, flinging herself to the ground and wrapping her arms around his strong neck and burying her face in his soft grey fur and breathing his smell that was forest and salt water and meat and fireside and all that was home and all that was hope and all that took away hunger and loneliness and fear.

'My wolf!' she sobbed. 'My wolf!' she laughed. 'My wolf! I thought you fell in spirit sleep! I sang your last spirit song! My ByMySide! Oh, my wolf! Where you been?'

'Mothga ...' said Daramurrum.

She lifted her face from ByMySide's fur and turned to Daramurrum crossly; this was a together time between her and her wolf. Daramurrum was not part of it.

'Mothga, look.' Daramurrum's voice was blue-cold. Fear-tipped. 'Look, Mothga. ByMySide's hurt.'

ByMySide looked at her and she at him. Mothgirl saw no pain in his amber eyes, only warmth and joy that they had found one another again. He licked her cheek. Surely Daramurrum was mistaken. Then Mothgirl noticed her wolf's legs; his two front legs were straight and strong as always, but his hind legs lay loose behind him on the dark ground. Mothgirl gasped.

'Oh, my wolf!' she whispered, rubbing his soft fur gently. 'Oh, my poor wolf! What has become of you?'

Gentle as a moth she felt around his back and hips; she found only one small wound, on his flank, but ByMySide made not a whimper.

'Maybe he's hurt his back?' said Daramurrum softly. 'My cat hurt his back once and his legs went all floppy too. But after some rest he was OK.'

'ByMySide oak-ee?' asked Mothgirl.

Daramurrum bit his lip. 'I'm no expert but, hopefully, I mean he's probably not stopped running around trying to find you since the moment he lost you. Now that he's here and you're here maybe he'll lie down and go to sleep and feel better ...' Daramurrum's voice faded away. Was he telling untruth? 'Hey, I think he's thirsty,' he said in a new, bright voice.

Daramurrum was telling truth about that; ByMySide's tongue lolled from his mouth as though he was hot, but even his panting was strangely quiet.

Taking something from his back bag, Daramurrum twisted the top of it and lifted it to his lips. Mothgirl heard the sound of his swallows and she licked her own dry lips.

'Water,' he said, holding the strange drinking gourd out to Mothgirl. She went to him, took it, drank how he drank, then poured water into her cupped hand. Her wolf lapped it quick-gone. Mothgirl went to Daramurrum for more.

ByMySide followed her to the yellow-thorn bush, dragging his unmoving hind legs behind him. The sight of him made Mothgirl's heart pang. What had happened to her wolf? Had he been struck by the Needle Rocks or swirled about in the Big Water like that broken black tree? Poor ByMySide.

Step. Step. Drag.

Step. Step. Drag.

Mothgirl and Daramurrum stared at each other, wide-eyed. It was a sound they had both heard before.

ACCCK-ACCCKK-ACCCK-accck. Mothgirl spun around.

A yellow-eyed gull on a black rock stared back at her. *Accck-accck-accck*, he cackled again before stretching his strong wings and setting flight.

Pouring water into her palm, Mothgirl crouched by her wolf. She sniffed the gentle familiar smell of him and in it was mixed that dangerous red tang of blood from his wound. Mothgirl looked her wolf in his sunrise eyes. 'It was not Vulture in the tunnel. It was you, ByMySide,' she whispered. 'It was you!'

ByMySide drank, then tossed his head. He opened his jaw as if he was barking an *Of course it was me!* answer, but, even though he made the movement, no sound came out.

'He's lost his voice!' said Daramurrum, crouching down too.

ByMySide made another soundless bark in response.

'Poor boy,' said Daramurrum, holding out his hand for the wolf to sniff. ByMySide gave his palm a lick and Mothgirl stared in half-jealous astonishment – he was *her* wolf; ByMySide did not share his licks widely.

'He lost his voice, but he not lost his nose,' she muttered.

'What do you mean?'

'ByMySide have strong, clever nose. He smell good spirit. He smell cruel spirit. He smell danger.' She shrugged and gave Daramurrum a small smile. 'My wolf like the smell of your spirit, Daramurrum.'

Daramurrum smiled back, stroking his hand over ByMySide's neck fur. 'Well, you can tell him from me that I like the smell of his spirit too.'

ByMySide barked a silent bark and they both laughed. Then her wolf rested his heavy, tired head in Mothgirl's lap.

Dara watched ByMySide sleep while Mothga stroked his fur. How did they end up here? How did he end up with them? Was it just a big crazy chance? Just luck?

Luck! For the first time since Dara got to the island he thought about the Golden Hare. He slid his hand deep into his pocket; to his amazement, his little brass hare was still there; he wrapped his fingers around the tiny pointy-eared shape and squeezed. The Golden Hare! '*Once, long long ago, when all our world was new …*' he murmured, feeling the familiar wave of longing and wonder and regret flood through him. He smiled to himself; he'd finally made it to Lathrin Island, but suddenly finding the Golden Hare wasn't all that mattered any more.

He glanced again at Mothga and at ByMySide. He'd found something even more extraordinary, and maybe that was even more lucky. But as Dara stared at ByMySide's poor hurt legs, he realised that the wolf still needed all the luck he could get.

A long low moan floated in the wind.

Mothga grabbed Dara's arm pinch-tight. 'What that?' she whispered.

Dara swallowed. 'I don't know.'

The moaning groan came again, and Dara glanced up fearfully at the banshee moon.

Then a shape came shuffling out of the shadowy pre-dawn.

And suddenly Dara remembered the dunes and he started to giggle with relief; he knew exactly what it was: 'It's only a cow!' he said, shining his torch across. The cow mooed again and slowly wandered away.

'Ow?' said Mothga, taking the torch and eying the cow suspiciously. 'That aurochs! Where her herd?'

'Oh, there are only a few cows kept out here now.'

'Who keep ows? How keep ows?'

'They're just left from when people lived out here; the islanders bred cows, you know, for milk and meat and stuff. And they grew their own wheat – look –' Dara pointed at the hollow of whispering silvery grass – 'that was one big wheat field a hundred years ago.'

'Eat field?' said Mothga in confusion.

Dara pulled the head off a stem of wheat that had

242

self-seeded right next to them. 'Wheat,' he said, pulling off the grains and offering them to her.

'*Eat*,' said Mothga, chewing one thoughtfully while picking at another with her nail. '*Eat field* ...' She scooped up the grains of wheat from Dara's palm; she slid them into her pouch and, pausing for a second, she took something out.

'Daramurrum?' she said. 'A bargain? I give you my fire stones. You give me your *water-poo-tosh*.'

'Deal!' said Dara. Mothga pressed the two flints into his hand and slid the torch into her pouch, looking very pleased with herself.

Dara laughed, rubbing the stones sparklessly together.

The cow mooed again. Further off this time.

FEARS

Mothgirl gently dabbed ByMySide's wound with healing paste from her pouch. She stroked his thick fur, over and over and over, deep-glad but sorrow-heavy.

'I ran from you, ByMySide,' she said, a guilt-stricken whisper in his soft flicking ear. 'I mistook you for cruel Vulture come to claim me through the dark. But you are you, ByMySide. You are you! You followed me. You never left me. And I … I closed the door on you, my dear wolf.' ByMySide sleepishly licked the tear from her cheek. She nuzzled her chin into him; his softness felt like home. 'I thought you were someone who you were not, ByMySide, and I feared you …'

She raised her chin and glanced over at the lynx-haired boy from the far-ice-lands. 'I feared you also, Daramurrum,' she said softly.

'You're pretty scary yourself, Mothga, when you want

to be,' answered Daramurrum with a smile. 'I guess we're all a bit afraid of things we don't know. Things we don't understand.'

'I feared your foot deerskins,' said Mothgirl gravely. 'I not understand your foot deerskins, Daramurrum.'

'You were afraid of my wellies!' Daramurrum laughed a snortish laugh. 'Here – try one on – face your fears.'

'Wellies!' Mothgirl giggled and slid her foot into Daramurrum's strange yellow foot deerskins. 'My foot like a na-na!' she laughed, wiggling her toes.

'You're a na-na!' said Daramurrum, offering her the other welly.

Mothga looked down at her strange yellow na-na feet and giggled until her laughter melted to a smile.

She gazed out over the Big Water – morning was coming and the sky was flame-tinged at one edge and star-tingled along the other. All that was strange seemed fearful, but was it truly? Perhaps fears melted like ice if you held them in your hand.

Mothgirl's eyes found the familiar shape of her Spirit Stone, rising up from its ring of amber-glow lights, far away across this strange and treeless land. 'Home,' she whispered. And she realised what she was most afraid of.

She was afraid to return home.

And not just because of cruel Vulture, but because she knew now that Hart had truly gone and she would need to stand strong alone and say to Pa, 'No, Pa. This is not the way.'

'*What is the way then, Mothgirl?*' Pa would answer, storm-voiced. '*What big new way ought things be done?*'

Mothgirl swallowed. '*Nor-mill is not the way,*' she whispered, and from somewhere on the island came the long lowing of the *ow*. Mothgirl gazed at the sky-tall hut made of strong stone and at the whispering *field of eat* and she felt new thoughts strike against each other in her mind, like fire stones making sparks.

Mothgirl shivered. She held her fears, like ice in her hand. 'I need go home, Daramurrum,' she whispered.

HOME

Dara nodded sadly. It was time.

'How?' Dara looked around the wind-ruffled clifftop for a … portal … or a window … or a … he-didn't-know-what. 'How do you do it? How do you get home, Mothga?' he asked.

Mothga's eyes lost their heaviness and their worry. She laughed a twinklish laugh, nudging him like he'd made a great joke. '*I* not know how get me home, Daramurrum!' She giggled. 'You from far-ice-lands! *You* know how get me home!'

Dara blinked at her in astonishment. 'I really don't, Mothga,' he said.

But that just made her laugh all the more.

Dara looked to the mainland. Tiny lights were already snaking along the main road to Mandel. Back at Carn Cottage, Mum and Dad would wake up soon; he bit his lip, picturing them whispering on the landing and then ignoring the *Do Not Disturb* sign and coming into his room and Dad opening the curtains and Mum whispering, 'Wake up, sleepy socks,' like she always did, and gently pulling back the covers ... to find a bed full of scrunkled-up Lathrin legends ... and no Dara at all.

A wave of guilt prickled through him. He winced. What had he been thinking? Mum and Dad would be so so worried – they only ever wanted to keep him safe.

He needed to go home too.

He turned to Mothga. She was watching him with a look he didn't understand; somewhere between curious and cross and pitying.

'You lost, Daramurrum,' she whispered, softly touching his arm. 'You lost.'

Dara blinked at her. How could he be lost? He knew exactly where he was.

They both turned as from far across the misty sea came the low mournful groan of a foghorn. Dara watched the hazy lights of a freight ship move heavy along the horizon, following an invisible line from port to port across the sea. Always knowing exactly where it was going, always knowing what was coming next.

'Maybe I *am* lost, Mothga,' he whispered. 'I've been waiting and waiting all my life to be ... someone else.

I've been waiting for the Big Op to change me and make me not just better, but *better*, you know?'

She looked at him blankly.

He searched for the words to make her understand. 'I wanted to be better … bigger … stronger … like Hart … like Vulture … *a big strong man.*'

She smiled, shaking her head. 'You not big strong man.'

He felt the stab of her words. 'I know.'

'*I* not big strong man!' she said in her 'big strong man' voice.

Dara couldn't stop a little laugh.

'ByMySide not big strong man.' She paused and giggled at her own joke, but then her face grew serious. She cupped her hand and whispered to him through the early morning light, like she was sharing a secret.

'Big strong man is not big strong man, Daramurrum.' And she shook her head, as if, even as she spoke, she was almost surprising herself with her own thoughts. 'Big strong man *is not* big strong man! Vulture is shrivelled, stinking untruth. Hart is sadness-small and broken. Pa is …' She snorted. 'Pa is too *Pa.*'

They both laughed. ByMySide stirred in his sleep.

'You not need change you,' said Mothga softly. 'You Daramurrum.' And she shrugged. As if it was as simple as that.

'But … I'm not,' whispered Dara softly, feeling like a fake and a fraud and a liar. 'I'm not who you think I am, Mothga. I don't have whatever great powers you think I have. I'm not from *Far Eyes Land*. I don't know how to get you home. I don't even know how to get *me* home.'

She shrugged again. Like nothing he could say would convince her. 'You Daramurrum,' she said again.

And he felt the warrior rumble in the way she said his name; he gazed out over the sea and the sky grown golden, streaked with strands of amber and flame.

'Look!' gasped Mothga. 'Porr-poss-iss!' And she pointed to the waters near the sea stacks where a whole pod of porpoises leaped and played, flipping and splashing and gleaming in the waves.

'Porr-poss-iss!' he whispered, awestruck in the glow of it. A sudden thought hit Dara: porpoises didn't know they were porpoises, did they? Porpoises didn't know how amazing they were. They were just … themselves. Like Mothga didn't even know she was from the Stone Age. And ByMySide didn't know he was a wild wolf. Even the Golden Hare didn't know she was rare or special or extraordinary. Perhaps Mothga really *could* see something in him that Dara didn't even know was there.

Dara stood and walked barefoot to the foot of the lighthouse. Away from the shelter of the gorse bush the wind had got up again; stretching his arms wide, he let it buffet and ruffle him, feeling the sting of salt spray on his cheeks. He opened his mouth and took a big fresh breath.

Then he felt the tickly prickle of someone watching him.

He glanced over at Mothga; her eyes were fixed on the porpoises as she knelt by the gorse bush, absently stroking snoozy ByMySide.

A wild whoosh of wind made his torn hoody billow like a flag. He squinted towards where the cliff dropped away to a secret tunnel; the heather shivered in the gusts, glowing purple in the early light. Dara surveyed the coastline and the golden sea for miles around. No one was there.

But still Dara could feel eyes upon him.

Heartbeat quickening, he turned slowly inland. Down in the sheltered dip between here and the ruined village the tall pale stems of wheat and grasses swayed, bending and straightening in the breeze. Was someone hiding there, crouched low, watching him?

Dara ran his eyes along the shifting waves of golden grass. He swallowed. The swish of the seed stalks. The whisperings of the wind. The crash of waves on the rocks below.

A rustle from behind him.

Dara spun around. And he gasped.

A hare. A hare with pale gold fur stood on her rear

251

legs only a few metres away. The hare watched Dara with blue eyes that looked almost … human.

Slow as slow, Dara reached his hand towards the hare. It was the hare from his book – the Golden Hare from the story. The hare stood still, like a statue set in metal, so still that Dara jumped with surprise when she blinked.

Dara stared at the blue-eyed hare and the hare stared at Dara. Time felt enormous. Eternal almost. Dara could feel the slow turning of the earth, and its heavy pull. He breathed in the air of the island, and as he blew out, the hare blinked once more, twitched her nose, turned tail and ran.

'Wait …' whispered Dara. But the hare had disappeared into the long grass as if she had never been there at all.

And Dara heard a scrambling from the gorse bush and a shout. Spinning, he saw Mothga leap to her feet and grab at her wolf. But ByMySide slipped through her fingers and, still hobbling, ran into the long grass, chasing the Golden Hare with predator's eyes.

'No!' yelled Dara. 'Stop!'

HARE

Mothgirl ran after ByMySide, calling his name. She charged fast as fast into the *eat field* and the long grass. Pathless she ran and until the stems were taller than she was and the light matched their colour, following the *fuffle-crash* of her fast-bounding wolf.

'Stop!' she cried. 'Stop!' That hare was a spirit creature, true as true; Mothgirl had glimpsed the flash of the hare's blue-sky eyes.

'ByMySide, stop!' she yelled as she ran, but still she heard the rush and the whoosh of her wolf through the dazzle-bright grass and the sound filled her ears and became wave-crash and wind-roar and heart-thud and her whole self spun with it, dizzy as Big Water, breathless and noisy and bright as bright, and the smells of salt fish and *na-nas* and hawthorn and kelp rushed through her air and she gulped and she felt her feet slide from beneath her and she stumbled and fell out of the long grass and on to a mossy soft patch of clear earth.

Mothgirl stopped still. On hands and on knees. Breathing sweet and dust-dry air.

Then Mothgirl lifted her chin and looked up; she was kneeling at the foot of Owl Rock. She pressed her palms to its coolness and walked her hands up and up, until she stood, still panting, leaning on the rock for strength. Mothgirl shielded her eyes from the bright amber morning and looked out.

'Oh!' she gasped, her breath catching in her throat, her knees crumbling beneath her. 'Oh!'

She clung to Owl Rock and stared out over the Great Plain, dust bright in the morning light and bursting with yellow-thorn. Mothgirl lifted one foot out of Daramurrum's yellow foot deerskin and she wriggled her toes on the mossy ground and she felt its softness, true as true beneath her.

Laughing in amazement, she gazed down the craggy slope of Lathrin Mountain, to where, at its foot, a small herd of aurochs grazed and the wide river merged with the Big Water in swirlish patterns beneath the surface, blue and green and brown.

She followed the river back with her eyes to Carn Hill and beyond; the water gleamed as it bent and twisted through deep green forest all the way to her own dear hill. Her own dear Spirit Stone. Her own dear home. Tears fell fast and hot down Mothgirl's cheeks.

Soft fur tickled the backs of her legs. 'My wolf!' she gasped. For he was with her, by her side.

Wiping her eyes with her arm, Mothgirl bent down and ruffled ByMySide's grey head. He stood on four paws; her heart soared. 'You oak-ee!' she whispered. ByMySide licked her nose.

She got to her feet; she was still wearing Dara-murrum's red deerskin that crackled when she moved.

'Daramurrum?' she whispered. And she peered around her at the dip in the mountaintop and the rocky cliffs beyond it. Gone was the *eat field* and the sky-tall, bright-light hut. Gone was the stone-hut camp down below. Mothgirl bit hard on her lip.

'Daramurrum?' she called, her voice a small squeak, lost in the whirling wind.

REAL LIFE

'Mothga!' yelled Dara into the swirling long grass. 'MOTHGAAAA! BYMYSIIIIDE! Where are you?'

Suddenly the wild wind stilled again. Like someone somewhere had just flicked a switch. Dara turned around and around; he couldn't see Mothga or ByMySide anywhere. He'd even lost their flattened trail in the grass.

'Mothgaaa!'

But the only answer was the roar of the waves at the foot of the cliffs and the squawk of the seabirds wheeling overhead.

Dara walked and called and searched, worry cold and heavy in his belly. What if ByMySide had run right off a cliff? And what if Mothga had tried to climb down to save him? Or what if they'd fallen down a tunnel shaft? Or what if ...

Dara stepped out of the long grass and to his surprise

he was standing in a little mossy clearing right up at Owl Rock.

He climbed the small slope slowly. Biting his lip, he peered over the edge at the crashing waves down below, but to his relief all he saw was dark rocks and whooshing wild water. He opened his backpack and took out his binoculars. Leaning on Owl Rock, he searched the cliffs and the sea and the island for a glimpse of a red raincoat or a flash of grey fur.

'Where are you, Mothga?' he murmured. Real people didn't just vanish into thin air. 'Real people ...' he whispered aloud, lowering his binoculars slowly. Because most real people nowadays didn't wear animal skins either ... or have wolves for friends ... or eat bananas skin and all. Dara bit his lip.

He felt babyish and pathetic and embarrassed. Like he had that time at school in Year 4 when Steffan Baxter told him that the Golden Hare wasn't real and was just made up and didn't exist and was impossible. He winced.

Everything that had happened had been impossible. He shook his head, like trying to shake water from your ears after a swim. Mothga was impossible. Had he just made Mothga up?

Dara leaned on Owl Rock; he ran his fingers over its cold, rough, sturdy not-made-up-ness.

Suddenly his fingertips stopped. Retraced their steps, felt the rock again.

Nose to stone, Dara peered at the surface of Owl Rock up close.

There was a shape etched there. It was ancient and faded but it was clear. He traced it again with his fingertip, softly.

A triangle. And another triangle. Meeting each other at their narrowest points. Like a little bow almost. Or like a pair of wings. A butterfly even. Or … a moth.

'Moth,' he whispered. 'Mothga!' Could this be – what had she called it back in the cave? A *waymarker*. Could this be Mothga's own waymarker? A sign to say that she had been here. A sign to stop her getting lost. A sign to help her find her way back home.

And as he traced Mothga's waymarker, a tingle passed from the rock to his fingertip and into his blood. A tingle like a pinch that showed he was not dreaming. That showed he was truly alive.

'Thank you, Mothga,' he said quietly, smiling warm and wide. He rested his palm over Mothga's waymarker and looked out over the wild waking sea.

He watched the squawking seabirds soar and swoop and bob and dive and bicker and settle. Who would ever have known how crazy-busy it actually was out here on deserted Lathrin Island at the crack of dawn? When he'd pictured it in his head it had all been still and quiet as a picture in a book, but *in real life* there was a puffin with sprats dangling from his beak like a silver moustache; in real life a gannet dropped into the sea with a dive so swift and smooth it took Dara's breath away; in real life an enormous, ominous black-backed gull perched on a rock, eyes peeled for prey.

In real life a Stone Age girl and a Stone Age wolf had walked upon this island, and he'd walked with them. It wasn't possible. But it was true.

Maybe there was more to real life than he ever could plan for. Maybe stuff he didn't expect or even imagine was waiting around every corner. Good stuff. Bad stuff. Strange, amazing, scary stuff. No one ever knew. There was no map. There were no answers.

'Lathrin Island,' Dara whispered, and he looked out at the huge sky that was night and was day both at once, at the sea that was deadly-dark and shimmerish-beautiful; Dara thought about impossible things and possible things, and how really they were all just the same.

Mothgirl slid her cutting stone back into her pouch. She pressed her hand to her waymarker. She closed her eyes. 'I give thanks, Daramurrum,' she whispered. For a moment the dark rock felt warm as touch and soft as skin beneath her palm.

Mothgirl rested her other hand on ByMySide's soft head. 'Home,' she murmured, opening her eyes, and she ran down the mountainside towards the river's edge and the Great Plain and the endless trees beyond.

As she ran she felt the extra weight of the *water-poo-tosh* bouncing in her pouch and she heard the soft rattle of the grains of *eat*; new ideas sparked and sparkled in her mind. Impossible ideas. Ideas that Pa and Hart and Vulture had never even imagined. Ideas that were *simply not the way*.

The aurochs herd scattered at the sound of her

running footsteps, so that when she reached the river all that was left were hoof prints in the mud. She dipped her hand into the river and was about to drink when she noticed the deer carcass.

The bones were spread all across the wide shallow river, picked dry by other creatures so there was no meat left on them for ByMySide, let alone for her. Still, she thought it best to drink from upwater.

As she drank she glanced at the deer skull. The jaw-bone had washed away but the antlers and the top-skull were all still there; she did a little shudder, looking at the empty eyeholes. Fearing the way they watched her back.

Quick-walking, Mothgirl moved away through the fast shallow water. Mothgirl wore her yellow foot deer-skins proudly – no river water touched her feet. It was like a strange spell; Eelgirl and Owlboy might even fear those yellow foot deerskins; fear them or want them, it would be one or the other.

Mothgirl froze in the moving water. *Fear.*

She glanced back at the deer skull, she stared down at her strange red Daramurrum deerskins; pulling up her hood, she gazed at her horrible, rippling, red reflection. These were things that Vulture had not seen before; impossible things. In her mind came the echo of Dara-murrum's words: *We're all a bit afraid of things we don't know. Things we don't understand.*

She remembered one of Pa's old firestories – The Spirit Beast, it was called, and it had always filled her heart with dread and shivers. She still heard Pa's firestory voice in her deep rememberings:

> *… and if you are cruel of hand, eye or tongue,*
> *then in darkest of nights the Spirit Beast comes.*
> *Half creature, half woman, the Spirit Beast sings,*
> *And with strange silent song, hunted creatures she brings.*

Mothgirl shuddered.

Then she smiled; another idea *tap-tap-tapped* inside her mind, like a chick trying to crack its way out of an egg.

Tap-tap-tap. Tap-tap-tap.

'There!' Dara said aloud. He blew the stone dust off Owl Rock and gazed admiringly at where he'd carved his very own waymarker, right next to Mothga's one.

A 'D' for Dara … and a shadow 'D' too for Dara-murrum. The one a reflection of the other. Two halves of the same thing.

He slipped his penknife into his backpack and ran his fingertip over the fresh-cut lines; maybe Mothga might come back to Lathrin Island one day, wondering if *he* was real. Dara smiled, imagining her seeing his way-marker and knowing that he *had* been here … and that he'd found his way.

Dara squinted out over Lathrin Strait; he could just make out the dim outline of Carn Cottage, huddled and cosy on the little hill behind the sand dunes. It looked so small from here; he pictured himself – a tiny face in a tiny window in that tiny cottage on the edge of that tiny seaside town.

Shutting his eyes, Dara imagined himself curled up cosy in his bed, with his head on his pillow, while his oxygen machine beeped and whirred comfortingly beside him. He imagined Mum stroking his hair and Dad calling him *son-shine* and Charlie perched cross-legged on the other bed reading *The True Legends of Lathrin Island* out loud to him for the thousandth time.

He needed his family.

He'd come out here to prove that he could do everything just fine on his own, thank you very much. But – Dara smiled – he'd actually proved totally the opposite: he needed other people. He needed people like Mothga – people who were kind and funny and not at all *nor-mill*. People who accepted him for who he was, and who needed him just as much as he needed them.

People like Mum and Dad and Charlie and Tam.

And he needed stories. Stories that were impossible … and true.

He ran his fingertip over his waymarker. *He* needed to accept who he was and stop fighting it, stop wishing to be someone he wasn't. Dara put his hand over his real-life heart. Mothga's green gloop was all dry and flaky now; he picked a bit of it off with his fingernail. One day he *would* have his Big Op, but when he did, the world wouldn't suddenly burst open, full of blossom and unicorns and shooting stars. After the Big Op he'd still be him; he'd still be himself always and forever – rubbish at some stuff, great at other stuff, just like everybody else. Everybody is kind of stuck with themselves really.

Dara grinned and sighed a slow sigh. He could feel a tightness in his breath that he didn't like but that he understood. He'd be able to take his morning tablets soon. 'Pink Pills of Power,' he muttered, and he bit his lip. It really was time to go home. Dara just wasn't sure exactly how.

Small lights moved in the harbour; fishermen probably – up early. Maybe he could shout and wave and they'd see him and come out to the island and rescue him.

Then he remembered Mothga and her lost brother. 'Make light and I will find you!' he whispered. That was it. He rummaged in his backpack for his torch. He could signal with it from up here at Owl Rock and they'd be sure to notice –

Oh. Dara remembered that he'd traded his *water-poo-tosh* for Mothga's fire stones. He took the two flints in his hand and looked at them. 'Not a good idea,' he muttered.

Out of the corner of his eye he saw the fishing boat

start to edge out of the harbour, taking the route between the buoys; he had no time to lose.

He tried to remember what Mothga had done. He gathered a small tangle of dry grass and put it on the mossy ground. Then, bending close over it, he struck and struck and struck the flints together.

STRANDED

Nothing. Not even the tiniest spark.

Dara looked up and saw the fishing boat start to pick up speed. *No!*

He struck the flints together faster and more frantically than ever. Suddenly a tiny spark leaped like a fairy from the flint to the grass. 'Yes!' hissed Dara, remembering what to do. Picking up the little nest of grass, he blew and blew on it until it smouldered and a tiny red glow shone out from the heart of it. He laid it on the ground again and fed the fire with thicker stems of grass now, sheltering the tiny fire from the wind with his hands. Smoke billowed and Dara looked for the fishing boat. It was nearly at the headland by Owl Rock.

'Hey!' he shouted, waving his arms. 'Up here! Help!'

Dara fed the little fire some more grass stems, but

when he looked back to the fishing boat it was already beyond the headland, with Owl Rock behind it.

'Come back!' cried Dara, waving as the boat chugged further and further out into the sea beyond the island.

Dara slumped down, leaning on Owl Rock, feeling the familiar clench of his chest. He was stranded.

From over at the harbour Dara heard the church bells *dong* seven o'clock. He shook his head, putting another twig on the fire. He'd give it till about 8.30 before Mum and Dad went into his room and found he wasn't there and worried themselves sick. He bit his lip guiltily.

They'd call the police. And the ambulance. And the fire brigade.

He'd have to sit out here on Lathrin Island with his stupid little fire, listening to the sirens, watching the blue lights flashing back on the mainland. What a mess!

Mum would be crying and Dad would be crying. They might even go on the news and do one of those awful interviews asking for help. The ones where when Dad watched them his eyes welled up and he said, 'Oh, those poor people.'

Dara felt like crying too, just thinking about it. But he didn't cry. He just sat still as still, leaning on Owl Rock, doing his breathing exercises and trying not to think about his heart that fluttered and flitted in his chest, nervous as a trapped bird.

268

He unzipped the pocket of his bag, had a puff of the puffer and slid it back in its place. Dara's head was swimming. He lay curled up on the soft moss and closed his eyes.

Dara didn't see the final wisp of smoke from his fire twist its way into the bright morning air.

Dara didn't see the white fishing boat turn in a churning circle in the glittering water and chug into the island's small harbour.

Dara didn't see a black-and-white collie called Mackerel come charging up to Owl Rock or feel her lick his face.

Dara didn't hear Mackerel bark and bark and bark until her owner caught up with her.

Dara didn't feel the fisherman press his big trembling fingers to Dara's wrist and feel for his pulse.

Dara didn't hear the fisherman's mumbled prayer as he turned and ran back like lightning to his boat and called *'Mayday! Mayday! Mayday!'* desperately into his radio.

CALF

Mothgirl walked into the cool green dark of the trees. The familiar smell of moss and leaf rot filled her and she smiled. She stopped walking and readjusted the deer skull she carried in her arms; it was heavy and the antlers tangled themselves in the creepers. Mothgirl rolled her eyes; how did deer ever manage to walk *anywhere* with these foolish things on their heads?

She heard a noise. She froze to listen; it was a soft, sad cry. ByMySide growled at the sound.

'Be still, my wolf,' she whispered. 'I need listen.'

The cry was coming from back on the fringes of the Great Plain; Mothgirl turned and peered back the way they had come. There, nestled in a hollow at the root of a tree, she could see a small furrish shape. She walked closer and the shape lifted its head and made its small sad cry again. It was an aurochs calf, left behind by the herd.

Mothgirl went to walk on. The aurochs calf would be too small for good eating; more bones than flesh. ByMySide pawed her leg; he made the small noise that spoke *Mine, Mothgirl. Mine! Mine!*

'You find your lost voice, my wolf – now that you are hungry! Go then, ByMySide! Eat your fill.' She tossed her head and ByMySide trotted back to where the calf lay. As she walked on, Mothgirl heard the small cry stop, and presently the footfalls of ByMySide padded along behind her once more.

But still the foolish antlers twisted themselves in vines and bracken. She paused for the eleventeenth time and glanced at ByMySide. Then she gasped, clapping her hand over her mouth.

A small laugh escaped her lips.

'What do you do, strange wolf?' she said, shaking her head.

ByMySide looked at Mothgirl shyly, then quick he looked away, for in his sharp white jaws was the aurochs calf. Unharmed. Asleep. ByMySide gripped him gently, as if he was a small small wolf cub.

'ByMySide!' smiled Mothgirl. 'Why you want that small small calf?' But as she asked the question she thought once more of the *ows* on the island and a brave new idea began to shape itself in her mind.

They walked together, following the path of the river, each carrying their own special burden. As she passed the cave where she had sheltered with Voleboy, Mothgirl peered into its darkness. 'Voleboy,' she hissed. But he was no longer there. A strange pang struck her and she was surprised by it. She sighed, wondering what would have become of them had she said yes to Voleboy's request to journey with her. Being Mothgirl alone felt natural then. But now, since Daramurrum, she felt an unfamiliar longing for the company of friends.

As Mothgirl drew closer to her home, her feet felt heavier and a sick sense of dread gnawed in the pit of her belly. Terrible possibilities writhed like vipers in her mind. Cruel-eyed Vulture was capable of horrors, she had known that since always. And Pa … She had disappointed Pa; she had not behaved in the way he believed was right; Pa might turn his back to her, not welcome her with warm arms. And Hart. Oh, Hart. She could not let herself forget that no matter how hard she had looked, she had not found her own lost brother.

She passed the rapids and after the rushing racket of their fast water she heard new noises in the stillness of the evening forest. Shouts came from high on the hill by the Spirit Stone. Mothgirl listened hard for the warm lilt of familiar voices.

But her heart turned sudden-cold. 'No!' she breathed, her voice just a small squeak as the forest echoed with the cruel *ACK-ACK-ACK* of Vulture's laughter.

Mothgirl felt her hands start to tremble. Another noise came then. The soft sad cry of the aurochs calf. 'ByMySide,' she whispered, stroking her wolf's soft head. 'This small small aurochs will fall to spirit sleep, dear wolf. He has no ma aurochs to give him milk.'

Her wolf laid the small creature down on the earth and went to drink from a river pool. Mothgirl watched as the aurochs calf followed ByMySide with his brown eyes, then stood on knobble-kneed legs and teetered after the wolf, taking shelter between his grey legs. Mothgirl sighed; she took pity and plucked milk flowers. Lifting the small warm calf in her arms, she fed them to him, one by one, until he slept once more.

'We need hide this calf,' said Mothgirl. She shuddered, knowing that if Vulture found him, he would surely drain the calf's blood to paint upon his own shrivelled face. So Mothgirl and ByMySide climbed to the clearing on the hill and tucked the aurochs calf into the hollow yew tree – a snug little nest.

Mothgirl glanced towards the Spirit Stone, to where a

thin lick of smoke drifted skyward. Darkness was falling; fish were sizzling; firestories were being told.

Taking a big breath, Mothgirl made fists of her hands as she summoned every scrap of her strength and courage. She was spearless. She was small. She was afraid. But she was stubborn as stone and full-spirit-bright. She had crossed the Big Water. She had walked upon Lathrin Mountain. She had seen things that would make Vulture and his men melt with fear.

Mothgirl had an idea. All that she loved most depended on it. She trembled.

'I oak-ee,' she whispered to herself. Then, stealthy as a shadow, with her wolf at her heel, Mothgirl crept towards her camp.

BEASTS

Mothgirl entered the grove and peeped between the branches. Home did not look like home. The fire blazed unruly, and upon the ground all around it lay bones and nutshells, discarded and unkempt. Two painted men crouched upon rocks by the fireside; Mothgirl could hear only fragments of their words: boasts of whose spear was the sharpest, whose arrow had made the most kills. She recognised their voices though; these were the men who had come hunting for her when she was hidden with Voleboy in the cave. She swallowed.

Where was her family? Away from the fireside all was shadows. Mothgirl squinted into the dark. Her heart leaped as she recognised the familiar skip of Eelgirl coming fast from the berry thicket. Mischievous, meddlesome, dearest Eelgirl! Joy rushed through Mothgirl so strongly she had to stop herself from running straight to

Eelgirl and wrapping her tight in her arms. Eelgirl ran to the fireside and Mothgirl suddenly noticed another figure seated there – a figure so thickly draped in furs that he resembled a bear more than a person. A shiver of fear and repulsion crept through Mothgirl's bones.

Vulture.

Mothgirl watched as Eelgirl knelt before him, her cupped hands outstretched.

His thin wheedling voice cut sharp through the evening air. 'What do you bring for Vulture, fool girl?' His shadowy shape leaned forward to peer into the child's hands.

'Gah!' He spoke through his teeth in small sharp stabs. 'You – bring – Vul-ture – six – small – bit-ter – berries!' He grasped Eelgirl's wrist.

Mothgirl winced, hearing her cry of pain.

'You have eaten all the sweet berries. You have feasted alone in the shadows.' His voice rose high into the night. 'And now you return to Vulture with THIS!'

'No, I … No, I …' Mothgirl's eyes clouded at the sound of poor Eelgirl's small small voice.

'Silence, thief!' Vulture flung Eelgirl away from him with such force that she fell sprawled on the dark ground, berries scattered all around.

Mothgirl had to bite her fist to stop herself from crying out in rage as Eelgirl sobbed and the painted men laughed their *ack-ack* laughs. Where was Pa? Why did he not stand tall and protect poor Eelgirl? Next to her ByMySide bristled, growling like thunder. 'Wait, my wolf,' she whispered.

'Viper, take this thieving fool girl to the others. Tie her tight with vines.'

One of the men rose and dragged Eelgirl away towards the Spirit Stone, kicking and biting and sobbing.

Mothgirl watched where he went. In dim of twilight she could just make out the shadows of Pa and Owlboy, tied tight to the Spirit Stone. Her heart thudded with fury and with fear.

'This night,' said Vulture, chin raised skyward. 'The moon is small and sharp. Let us quell the flames of our fire here so the beasts have nothing to fear. Let us lead the beasts here with blood trail. They will come. Bare-toothed. Sharp-clawed. And we shall let them come. We shall invite them to a fine feast.'

'ACK-ACK-ACK,' cackled the painted man, his greasy face shining red in the firelight. 'ACK – ACK. A fine feast of ... EAGLE ... and EEL ... and OWL! ACK-ACK-ACK.'

'Yes,' said Vulture slowly. Mothgirl could hear the sneer in his voice. 'For we are cunning. And as the beasts feast we shall stick them with our spears and shoot them with our arrows.'

'Ah – the plenty!'

'Yes – the great plenty!'

Mothgirl could bear to hear no more. With her hand tight on ByMySide's fur, she turned and crept silently away.

She reached the clearing and crawled into the tiny tree hollow with ByMySide and the calf. Here she wept. Trembling hopeless tears. She had no weapon. She had no clan. She had no chance. Her family had been taken and her plan had crumbled like sand. She had been a fool to believe that she could trick grown men's spirits into terrors. Ha! She could not make these painted men fear her and flee when her very own heart was so heavy with terror.

As Mothgirl wiped her eyes with her hand she saw that ByMySide's ears were pricked and alert. 'What hear you?' she whispered, quiet as breath. And then she heard it too; footfalls were creeping through the forest towards them.

STEALTH

The small small aurochs calf wriggled in Mothgirl's arms. *Do not wake! Do not cry out! Not this moment, please!* thought Mothgirl.

But the calf's hunger was noisier than his tiredness. His cry sailed out into the night air. The soft rustle of footfalls stopped. Mothgirl held her breath.

The small calf fell suddenly silent, like he too held his breath, like he too listened. Then with a squirmish leap he released himself from Mothgirl's hold and he ran from the safety of the hollow tree off into the night. Before she could stop him, ByMySide followed too.

Alone in the tree hollow, Mothgirl's heart made music in her ears as she tried to listen. For a long moment all was still: only wind and leaf whisper. Then came the sound of footfalls once more, but now they were no longer creeping and cautious but bold and ever closer. *Swoosh-swoosh. Swoosh-swoosh.*

Someone was standing in the clearing. Mothgirl could see him silhouetted in the moonlight. He, with the wolf and the calf at his side.

'Voleboy?' she whispered, emerging from her hiding place.

'Mothgirl!' he said. 'Your wolf told me you were returned. I called him to me with my bone whistle.'

Voleboy shared with her his gathered vine fruits and told her of Vulture's cruel doings while she had been gone. Heartsore, Mothgirl spoke in a trembling voice of Vulture's blood-trail plan.

'My father shames me,' said Voleboy. 'This is why I can no longer be his son. I would rather sleep alone and spearless in the rain than live within my father's hut.'

Mothgirl blinked. She had thought of Voleboy only as small and weak. She looked at him anew with Daramurrum eyes. He was not a *big, strong man* in body, but Voleboy's doings were courage-deep. It took great courage to have a strong thought and act upon it. Once Voleboy had asked if he could join her, but she had only known alone then; now she knew that the only way they could fight Vulture would be if they fought together.

Voleboy and Mothgirl together made a plan.

BLOOD TRAIL

Mothgirl and Voleboy watched from high in the yew's branches as Vulture's men spread the blood trail through the trees to the camp to the Spirit Stone, where poor Pa, Eelgirl and Owlboy were twined, together and weeping. Mothgirl's face was tight with fury as the men splashed her family's arms and legs with blood.

The men crept with spears and arrows within the shelter of the hut. Where was Vulture? This she could not see.

But the blood trail was set; they did not have long to act. Voleboy cleaned his bone whistle. And Mothgirl made ready. If she was going to succeed she would need to banish all softness from her heart. She would need to fill herself with menace from toenail to hair tip. She would need to be the red red Spirit Beast, ember-hearted and empty-eyed – with powers to tear stars from the skies and flood all the land with deep black water. Mothgirl took a big fierce breath. She nodded to Voleboy and lifted the hood of Daramurrum's red deerskin.

Together they crept through the grove, and on the fringes of the tree shadows Mothgirl raised the antler mask to her face and peered through the dark empty holes where the deer eyes had been. She felt inside the deerskin for the little pocket, and within it she flicked the switch of the *water-poo-tosh*. The light glowed upon her heart, red as blood through the deerskin, and Mothgirl walked out of the trees, chanting far-ice-lands words, low and ominous as thunder.

She heard the deerskins of her hut shift and she saw the frightened eyes of the men peep forth.

'Vulture!' came a trembling call. 'Vulture!'

From the shadows and the gloom came the soft cruel voice of Vulture. 'Spirit! Come! Vulture welcomes you here!'

Mothgirl's humming faltered slightly. She had not been expecting this. What should she do?

At that very moment she heard the first scuffling from tree shadows. An eagle, pale-headed, dark-eyed, swooped down from the near moonless sky. Voleboy's silent bone-whistle song was working! Mothgirl raised her arm and the eagle settled upon it; she had to hold back a gasp at the sheer wonder of it, although behind her antler mask she winced at the tight grip of the eagle's yellow claws and the strong-heavy weight.

'Welcome, oh spirit of the night.' Vulture's voice was higher now. Why was he not afraid? From within the hut she could hear the men's soft sobbing.

The sky whistled once more with flight and Mothgirl steadied herself as upon one of her great antlers landed a fine snow-white owl, whose yellow eyes watched Vulture unblinkingly. He rose and walked slowly towards them, hunched in his bearskin. Mothgirl ceased her humming, fearing he would come too close and know her for what she truly was.

Voleboy was watching closely; it was time to play upon his bone whistle, the strangest strongest song of all.

Wolfsong.

From the tree shadows stepped ByMySide, grey-furred, amber-eyed, magnificent. He stood between Mothgirl and Vulture.

Then there came rustlings in the bracken and shiverings in the brambles and tremblings in the briars and from the trees all around there came wolves. Not wolves who followed the blood trail but wolves who followed the wolfsong. They gathered around Vulture in a circle which closed ever tighter.

Mothgirl noticed his head turning from one to the other to the other, his eyes wide with panic now. 'Oh, kind spirit,' he said, thin-voiced. 'Oh, kind spirit, I am a but a humble hunting man, do not close your wolf pack upon me. Have mercy.'

From the hut Mothgirl saw the shadows of two painted men flee into the forest.

Vulture fell upon his knees. Mothgirl knew what she had to do. She peered at him through the spirit mask and bored her staring eyes deep within his skin. She bored deep into his cruelty and dug at it, loosening it like a root. Then Mothgirl threw back her head and she howled. ByMySide howled with her, and one by one the wolves all around howled too until the forest dark was heavy and aching with howls that heaped the song of togetherness upon the greedy ears of one.

ByMySide went to where Vulture lay trembling. With a short sharp tug, he tore the bearskin from him and tossed it aside.

There was nowhere to hide now. Shrivelled, wizened as a crab apple, his blood paint streaked with sweat and tears, Vulture became his own truth at last. He was powerless; he was just a man.

'Let me go,' he whispered. 'Let me leave this place alive, oh great Spirit Beast, and never shall my feet return. I promise you, upon my waking days and my spirit sleep.'

Mothgirl raised her arms high, trying to hide their trembling. At her signal, Voleboy gave one last silent screech upon the bone whistle. It was the music that spoke *Hunt!* within all the creatures' songs. So the owl and the eagle and the wolves whirled at Vulture as he ran in terror through the night. And was gone.

THE WAY

Mothgirl ran as fast as she could beneath the weight of her mask. She swiped her cutting stone and swiftly released Pa, Owlboy and Eelgirl. The small ones sobbed and buried their eyes in terror within Pa's deerskins.

Pa hobbled forward and fell to his knees. Filthy and hungry and broken and bruised.

Mothgirl's heart panged to see him so; behind her antler mask her eyes were wet with tears.

Pa offered the hand of peace to the Spirit Beast. 'Good Spirit Beast, I give thanks. You have saved us. I wish I had gifts to give you: fine bone knives, deerskins, meat – but Vulture has taken all that we had. So take my words and know that I speak with true tongue. We shall sing of you in firestories, good Spirit Beast, until the sun sleeps without waking.'

Mothgirl lowered her mask and laid the heavy antlers

upon the earth. Pa staggered back a step, staring, wide-eyed, speechless.

Then he opened his big arms as wide as the world and wrapped his daughter round. Mothgirl heard Eelgirl's cry and Owlboy's shout as they ran to join them, squashing their small bodies in alongside, like how cubs nuzzle into their pack. They stood like this for the longest while, all their faces soaked with tears.

'Where you go, Mothgirl?' asked Eelgirl. But Mothgirl would tell it in firestories all through the winter. Now was not the moment.

'Who that?' asked Owlboy, cowering behind Pa's legs. He pointed at Voleboy, who lurked shyly on the edge of the trees.

'Ah,' said Mothgirl. 'That Voleboy. He my friend. He come join our clan, Pa.' She spoke it like it was not a question. Like it was simply the way. Pa looked at Mothgirl, long and strong. With a warm eye twinkle he nodded.

Sometimes change was good.

But sometimes change was not good also.

'Hart?' whispered Mothgirl, pale with the weight of her own wondering.

Pa shook his head, sad and weary.

Mothgirl's heart crumbled. She looked to the pale stars and thought of her lost brother, her eyes all blurred with tears. Nothing ever stayed the same.

They walked together to the river, to wash the stinking blood paint from their skin. Owlboy wore one of Mothgirl's yellow foot deerskins and Eelgirl wore the other. Voleboy held them by their hands as they stood one-legged in the shallows and marvelled at their still-dry feet. Mothgirl told Pa of her plans for a hut of stone and a field of *eat* and an aurochs herd of their very own so that they could make this place a home all the year long. Pa was surprised. It was not a thing that was done … but he liked it.

The forest birds began to sing and the first beams of gentle sun were tingeing the sky palest blue; the others left the riverside and climbed back to their camp. Mothgirl stopped with ByMySide while he drank; she thought, unforgetting, of Daramurrum; of leaping por-poss-iss and a sky-eyed hare; of sprinkled stars upon the earth and of deep dark waters on the plain; she thought of all the impossible things and marvelled at the truth of them.

Mothgirl smiled; she knew that in the far-ice-lands Daramurrum would be awake and watching his own pale sun rising, remembering her too.

Mothgirl closed her eyes and listened while her world awoke.

From downstream Mothgirl heard a sound: the faint *plash-plash*ing of oar in water. Her heart soared – could it be … ?

Mothgirl ran fast along the riverbank, through trailing leaves and morning mists, until she rounded the river bend and there, just beyond the stepping stones, was a canoe nosing towards her through the clear water.

She let out a cry. A sun-sparkled cry of joy and wonder. For standing in the canoe was her very own dearest brother. Hart.

When he saw Mothgirl, Hart roared with joy. He leaped from his boat and ran splashing through the water towards her.

They stood in the fast, clear river, arms wrapped tight around one another, hearts bursting with firestories, impossible and true.

STORIES

Dara stood knee-deep in the frothy water and peered out over the wild grey sea to Lathrin Island. He listened hard, hoping to catch even the smallest hint of a howl looping through the whoosh of the wind.

But no. Only ordinary noises, *nor-mill* noises: the calls of seabirds; the giggles of children; the distant *moooo* of a cow grazing in the dunes. And another sound: the *crunch-crunch crunch-crunch* of footsteps running towards him across the sand.

Dara spun around.

'It's only me!' said Charlie, splashing through the waves. 'Just to warn you, Mum and Dad are still watching you from the window, so if you're planning on swimming over to Lathrin Island like the Golden Hare, then right now is probably not a very good idea. Maybe wait till after your Big Op this time.'

'Hi, Charlie.' Dara laughed. He waved up at Mum and Dad. 'They've been hovering over me like hawks ever since I got out of hospital,' he sighed, and he took a puff of his inhaler.

'Can't say I blame them, you nutball,' said Charlie, with a grin. 'When I heard what happened I ran out of work so fast my trainers were practically on fire – you ran off to a deserted island in the middle of the night! Who knows what you're capable of next?'

Dara nudged Charlie in the ribs.

'Oi!' said Charlie, dodging away. 'Seriously though, Dara, what were you doing out there?'

Dara let his eyes drift to where Charlie was pointing, across the grey water to Lathrin Island. What *had* he been doing out there?

When he'd first woken up in Mandel Hospital, he'd been so confused and groggy he'd thought he'd dreamed the whole thing. It all felt made up and ridiculous like a story. But now that he was back here by the swirling wild mysterious sea, Dara didn't feel so sure any more.

He bit his lip. Fingers of golden sunshine stretched through the cloud, making the gorse on the island glow yellow and the heather thrum violet. Dara thought about the lines, thin as mist, between possible and impossible, between real and not real, between here and now and there and then.

He closed his eyes, and in his own dark he saw leaping porpoises and sleeping seals, a hidden tunnel and a golden squawking daybreak. And he saw a girl dressed in deerskins and an amber-eyed wolf.

Dara peeped at Charlie out of the corner of his eye. 'You wouldn't believe me if I told you!'

'I might,' said Charlie with a little smile. 'I've got some pretty unbelievable true stories of my own, you know.'

Dara smiled back, and they walked together along the fringe of the sea, telling each other impossible things.

When they reached the end of the strand, Charlie slipped into the sea to swim and Dara sat on the rickety jetty, letting his legs swing over the water, looking back at their footprints in a trail along the sand: his own, and Charlie's, and deep deep beneath them, he knew there were Mothga's footprints in his yellow wellies, and ByMySide's paw prints too.

Dara squinted over at the Old Boatshed; the door was firmly shut and the only sign of life was a grumpy-looking gull perched on the roof.

So Dara turned away and, opening his backback, he took out a book; the dark blue cover was a swirl of stars, and within it was a sellotaped wodge of the once-crumpled pages he'd smoothed flat again and stuck back together. Dara traced his fingers over the silver loops of the letters, as if they were waymarkers carved into stone.

'*The True Legends of Lathrin Island,*' whispered Dara. He opened the cover and gazed at the map – ragged and weather-worn and still smelling faintly of woodsmoke. He turned the pages carefully, smiling at the stories like they were old friends: 'The Secret Smuggler', 'The Owl Rock', 'The Golden Hare' … until he reached the very back of the book.

Dara ran his hand across the first of the empty pages that he'd stuck in there too; he was ready.

The Way to Impossible Island, wrote Dara at the top of the smooth blank page.

And he began his own story.

ACKNOWLEDGEMENTS

No book is an island, and this one would have been an impossibility without a whole causeway of extraordinary people who have supported, guided and inspired me. As Mothgirl would say, I give thanks …

To my kind, wise and utterly wonderful editor, Lucy Mackay-Sim, who, like a lighthouse, has calmly and patiently led this story through mists of befuddlement and stormy seas. Lucy – you are a beacon of hope and loveliness!

To everyone in the Bloomsbury constellation – the shining stars who have guided this book on its way, most especially: glittering Bea Cross, sparkling Jade Westwood, glimmering Fliss Stevens, twinkling Jessica White, shimmering Sarah Baldwin, gleaming Nick de Somogyi, and a particularly enormous thank you to brilliant Cerrie Burnell for such a thoughtful, nuanced sensitivity read and for making my heart sing with kind comments.

To Ben Mantle for the impossibly beautiful cover art and to Patrick Knowles for the wild, windswept lettering and chapter-heading illustrations. You've both captured the spirit of Lathrin Island so perfectly.

To my agent, Nancy Miles, who is always there in sunshine or storm and who I absolutely treasure.

To all those who build bridges between books and readers: booksellers, librarians, literacy charities, teachers, bloggers, reviewers. The extraordinary tide of support you've given me in my first year as a published author really has meant so very much – thank you for planting wild green Stone Age forests in your bookshops, websites, classrooms and libraries.

To all the authors who have supported me in my debut year and welcomed me aboard. Particular thanks to my trusty crew of Bath Spa pals, my Scoobie shipmates and those wonderfully raucous Swaggers – I simply couldn't row, row, row this boat without you all!

To the real-life wolf pack at the Wild Place Project in Bristol: Forty, Socks, Faolin and Loki – I learned so much through watching you. Thank you also to your amazingly knowledgeable human, Zoe Greenhill, for answering even my most ridiculous questions, and to Jenny Stoves for arranging my visit. ByMySide became himself thanks to you.

To my friends and family for all the adventures we share – past, present and future. Thanks for the different shoes, the moonlight swims, the crumpled cottages, the waterfall giggles, the surprising daffodils, the unclosed gates, the birthday days, the mouse in the snow, the key in the mud, the alphabet of pebbles and the fox in the night. Thank you for letting me explore the world with you, and for all your endless support and love.

To Mum, for raising me on stories, flowers, kindness, creativity, laughter and tolerance.

To Dad and Anna, for taking us to real-life Lathrin Island and for all the joys of a sea-swept, storyful childhood.

To Amy, Alice and Niall for the wave-leaping, rock-pooling, sand-dune-rolling and general carrying on – thanks for all the stories we share.

To Sylvia and Peter for the 'writing retreats' by the sea; so much of this book was written at your lovely house and I'm very grateful indeed for your hospitality, kindness and company.

To my own wolf pack – Andrew, Lyla, Arlo and Flora – sharing a den and a life with you is the most wild and wonderful delight. Thanks for letting me sail off to impossible islands and for welcoming me home. Thanks for being dreamers and adventurers. Thanks for being by my side. I love you always.

And finally, dear reader, to you. When you read, you're part of the story; thank you with all my heart for being part of mine.

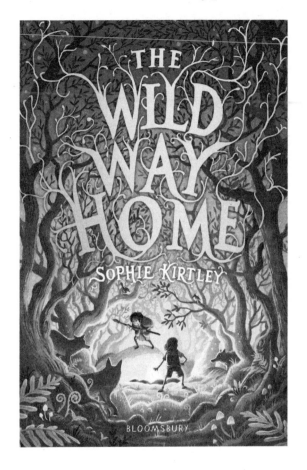

HUNT

I hide on the mossy branch of the hazel tree, my legs dangling into nothing. I wait. The wind rustles the leaves; a wood pigeon coos; the forest creaks and cracks like old bones.

A wordless shout. From the direction of Deadman's Cave. The Hunters are coming.

I squint into the hazy sunlight; I can see a ripple of trembling trees where they carve and smash through the forest. The crack-thump-rip of sticks grows louder as they tear their way closer and closer to my hiding place.

The Hunters hack through the bracken and out into the patch of sunshine, right at the foot of my tree.

It's them.

Lamont. Beaky. Nero.

I don't dare breathe.

Lamont stands, hand on hip, and peers into the forest. Beaky circles the tree, jabbing at rabbit holes, prodding the undergrowth with a long, sharp stick. Nero growls, black ears pricked, hackles raised, nose to the ground.

My heart thuds hard and loud.

Nero stops. He sniffs and lifts his nose towards me.

Then Nero turns his head sharply away. He can hear something, something else. Then I hear it too: there's rustling in the bracken.

Nero looks to Lamont. Lamont lifts a finger to his thin lips. Beaky nods.

They think the noise is me.

The thing in the undergrowth rustles again.

Lamont signals a countdown with his fingers:

Three.

Two.

One.

The Hunters charge into the bushes, yelling, their sticks raised high.

A young deer bounds out on the opposite side, tail pale amongst the tree shadows. It springs away and is gone.

Nero chases after the deer, barking.

'NERO!' yell Lamont and Beaky, waist-deep in a tangle of brambles.

I see my chance.

I touch wood, just for luck, then I scramble from my tree and I run.

Beaky shouts, 'It's Charlie!'

But I don't look back. Down the hill, through the forest, towards the river. My feet pound the ground and my fists pummel the air. I charge over the wooden bridge, and up the steep gravel path on the other side. Each breath is heavy. My chest hurts. At Druid's Well, I swerve off the path and run straight up through the bracken. I know exactly where I'm going.

I hear the thump of the Hunters running across the bridge. They're gaining on me.

I pass the rope swing and run through the patch of wild mint until I reach the edge of the clearing. Panting, I look back over my shoulder: all clear. I run out of the tree cover and up the mound, tugging on tufts of grass to heave myself right up to the top.

I reach the Spirit Stone and I lean with my forehead pressed on to the cool grey rock.

'Home!' I say, high-fiving the Spirit Stone.

Slumping down on to the grass, I close my eyes and gasp air into my aching lungs.

I won the game.

Nero reaches the Spirit Stone next. He just stands there panting. Lamont and Beaky don't bother running the last bit, not once they know I've beaten them. Lamont clambers up the mound and flops down next to me.

'Close one, Charlie,' he says. 'That deer put us off.'

'Just you blame the deer,' I say. Lamont does a little half-laugh and pokes me in the side. Nero comes over, long tail wagging, his eyes on the stick in his owner's hand.

'Go get it, Nero.' Lamont tosses the stick into the clearing. Nero charges all the way back down the hill again.

'Oi!' yells Beaky, still staggering up the mound. 'You nearly got me with that stick, Lamont!' When Beaky finally reaches the Spirit Stone she collapses beside us, breathing hard. 'Next time,' she pants, 'there's absolutely – no – way – I'm being – a Hunter – that forest is far – far –' she swallows – 'far too big – to find – anyone – in.'

'Just you blame the forest, Beaky,' I say. We all laugh, even Beaky.

We sit there, saying nothing, gazing out over our forest. I look at the gleaming river; I follow its twists and bends all the way through the forest, right out to where it widens and becomes the distant silver haze of the sea. I look at the far-off farmland cut neatly into green rectangles of fields, like slices of cake. I look at the town, how it spreads greyly up from the riverbanks, surrounding our forest, which surrounds this clearing, which surrounds this mound, which surrounds the Spirit Stone. *Home.* If I stretch my neck, I can just about see the roof of my actual home, where Dad is probably making tea for poor Mum, still stuck in bed waiting for the baby who'll be born soon.

STONES

The baby was supposed to come three days ago. 'D-Day,' Dad called it.

Mum's been counting the days off on the kitchen calendar with a big red pen; she's not been well so the doctors put her on 'bed rest' last month and it's driving her absolutely bananas. I breathe in the warm summer air, watching a flock of noisy swifts flit and swoop in the clear blue sky. I wouldn't be able to stand it either, being stuck inside in summer, not able to do anything fun at all. It'll be worth it in the end though. A little tingle creeps up my spine; soon I'll have a brother or a sister, and everything will change.

The light has that golden tinge now and the shadows are stretched. I take a smooth pebble out of my pocket.

Squinting up at the Spirit Stone, I move the pebble back and forward in the air, taking aim at the Spirit Stone's pointy peak.

Beaky sits up on her elbows to watch. I fling the pebble; it arcs up and over the Spirit Stone.

'Missed!' calls Beaky, flopping back down.

'Don't eat stones, Nero!' shouts Lamont as his dog charges off to find the pebble. Seconds later Nero's back, crunching away.

'Wow! He really listens to you, Lamont,' I say, in fake admiration.

'Shut up,' says Lamont, wheedling the pebble out from Nero's jaws. 'Do you want this back? Maybe add it to your collection?'

I laugh. 'No thanks. You can keep it, Lamont.'

'It's not just a *collection*, it's *Mandel Museum*!' says Beaky in a posh voice.

'I haven't called it that since we were in Year Two, Beaky!' I protest, laughing.

She ignores me. 'And that slobbery old stone's not quite weird enough. What's it going to look like next to the badger skull, and the arrowhead and the bird's nest, and the ...' Beaky lies there and lists all the things I've collected from the forest since we were little. Her eyes are shut and her long red hair is spread out on the grass. Lamont balances Nero's wet pebble on her forehead. Beaky shuts up, sits up and thumps him. I laugh again.

The evening sun is warm on my face. Shutting my eyes, I stroke Nero's silky soft ears. I sigh. I really ought to go home. Check on Mum. See if I've got a brother yet … or a sister.

'I'm off,' I say, standing up. 'See you tomorrow.'

'… for your birrrthdaaay!' sings Beaky. 'I can't wait! D'you think you'll finally get a phone, Charlie?'

'Maybe,' I say, crossing my fingers behind my back.

'Are we still camping out tomorrow night?' asks Lamont.

'Of course we are,' answers Beaky, before I even have a chance to think about it. Nero wags his tail like he's in agreement.

I pat Nero's black head. 'I guess it depends on the baby.' My shrug turns into a little shiver of excitement.

'Maybe baby!' grins Beaky, nudging me in the ribs.

I grin back. 'I'd better go.' I scramble to my feet. 'Bye!' I yell over my shoulder as I turn and run back down through the clearing and on to the gravel path through the forest.

Among the trees the air tastes cool and shadowy. The

branches on either side of the path lean in slightly, so it's dark like a tunnel. I can still hear the faint echo of Lamont and Beaky's laughter. A big clumsy bird flaps out of a tree, so close to my head I duck. My foot skids out in front of me and I end up sitting on the path. The bird lands on a branch, beady eyes staring at me. It's a wood pigeon with feathers the colours of early morning sky: grey and pink and silver.

I look down at the gravel I disturbed when I slipped. One small, pale stone catches my eye. I pick it up and rub it on my shorts to clean it. It's whitish, smooth, about the size and shape of an almond. I stare at the dull gleam of the stone on my muddy palm, and I realise it's not a stone at all. It's a tooth! A little shiver tingles like a breath across my shoulder blades.

A tooth, root and all! Wow! And it's not small either, must be from quite a decent-sized animal – a badger? A fox maybe? Or a deer? I don't care if Beaky and Lamont tease me about it; this tooth is definitely going in my collection. I've never found a tooth in Mandel Forest before. I get to my feet, pressing the tooth's pointy end into my fingertip; it leaves a little dimple there. I slide it into my pocket.

I feel the weight of someone watching me.

'Lamont? Beaky?' I call. It would be just like them to sneak up on me, get revenge for not winning the game.

There's no one here.

The wood pigeon in the tree ruffles his feathers noisily and I nearly jump out of my skin. 'You scared me!' I say as I gaze up at him. His feathers shimmer, swirling colours of oil on water.

The wood pigeon stares back. 'Whooo?' he says, his head cocked to one side. 'Whooooo? Whooooooooooo?'

I laugh.

'I'm Charlie Merriam,' I reply, and the wood pigeon flaps off.

Chollie. Murr. Umm, says a low voice from high in the tree behind me. A human voice. A voice I do not know.

I run. Faster than I've ever run before. Because this time it's not a game.

ABOUT THE AUTHOR

Sophie Kirtley grew up in Northern Ireland, where she spent her childhood climbing on hay bales, rolling down sand dunes and leaping the raw Atlantic waves. Nowadays she lives in Wiltshire with her husband, three children and their mini-menagerie of pets and wild things. Sophie has always loved stories; she has taught English and has worked in a theatre, a bookshop and a tiny pub where folk tell fairytales by candlelight. Sophie is also a prize-winning published poet.